AND THE
RAINBOW RANGERS

Also by
LAURA ELLEN ANDERSON

AMELIA FANG

AND THE
RAINBOW RANGERS

LAURA ELLEN ANDERSON

DELACORTE PRESS

For Dad. The true king of the "dad joke."
Thank you for being you and always encouraging
me to boldly go into my creative future.
Love you long and prosper! xxx

Text copyright © 2020 by Laura Ellen Anderson
Jacket art copyright © 2020 by Laura Ellen Anderson
Lettering and backgrounds © 2020 by Sarah Coleman

rhcbooks.com

Educators and librarians, for a variety of teaching tools,
visit us at RHTeachersLibrarians.com

Library of Congress Cataloging-in-Publication Data is available upon request.
ISBN 978-0-593-17249-0 (trade)—ISBN 978-0-593-17250-6 (ebook)

The text of this book is set in 13-point Cosmiqua Com Light.
Book design by Katrina Damkoehler

Printed in the United States of America
10 9 8 7 6 5 4 3 2 1
First American Edition

CONTENTS

THE SUGARPLUM TREE

BUGGINGTONSHIRE

MINIOPOLIS

LITTLE LAKE

SUGARPLUM ISLAND

THE EMPTY CAVES

THE SEA OF SPARKLES

DOCKS

SPARKLE SPA

LEPRECHAUN LAGOON

Ghoulish Greetings!

AMELIA FANG

AND SQUASHY

LIKES:
Hanging out with friends
Pumpkin Paradise Park!

DISLIKES:
Mean creatures
Tidying up her bedroom

TANGINE

LIKES:
His special eyelid cream
New clothes

DISLIKES:
Running out of eyelid cream
Being hungry

AND PUMPY

FLORENCE

LIKES:
Boat races
Foraging for food

DISLIKES:
Tangine's eyelid cream
obsession
Being called a beast

GRIMALDI

LIKES:
Being with his friends
His trusty scythe torch

DISLIKES:
What's in the Sea of Sparkles
Tragic stories

GRAHAM

LIKES:
Telling tragic stories
Sandwiches with extra filling

DISLIKES:
Ricky's map reading
Running out of tea bags

RICKY

LIKES:
The Rainbow Ranger club
summerhouses

DISLIKES:
Graham's tragic stories
Graham's driving

FRANKIE

LIKES:
His Nectar Carriage
His bug kingdom

DISLIKES:
Anything with butter
An unhappy bug

LIKES:
Being the best in class
Tormenting Amelia Fang

DISLIKES:
Amelia getting better grades
Being nice

KING JAMIE VII

CHAPTER 1

SPARE UNDIES

As the sun rose in the Kingdom of the Dark, the creatures of Nocturnia were all getting ready for bed—all except one little vampire and her pet pumpkin, Squashy.

"Moooom!" Amelia Fang called up the spiral staircase of the Fang Mansion. "Have you seen my pumpkin backpack? I need it for the Rainbow Rangers camping trip, and I have to be in Central Nocturnia Graveyard in ten minutes to meet everyone!"

A yellow door halfway down the corridor burst open and Countess Frivoleeta, a beautiful vampiress with VERY tall hair, appeared. She was wearing a long, sparkly

bathrobe with HUGE shoulder pads, and her hair was wrapped up in a glittery towel.

"Darkling!" she oozed, scooping Amelia up in her arms. "I can't believe you're going away for the *whole* half-moon break!" She kissed Amelia three times on each cheek, leaving behind shiny black lipstick marks. "Now, did you remember your fang polish? How about your pale-skin scrub? Oh, and some spare pairs of undies just in case any get eaten by vultures or something . . ."

"Mom!" Amelia blushed. "None of my things will get eaten by vultures. Plus, we're going to the Kingdom of the Light. You don't really get any vultures over there. And I need to find my pumpkin backpack or I won't be able to pack a spare pair of *anything*."

The countess thought for a moment and then disappeared into her bedroom. A few seconds later, she emerged from another room farther along the corridor. The doors of the Fang Mansion were rather unusual—they moved around whenever they pleased. Amelia was lucky if her bedroom was behind the same door for more than a few weeks at a time. Some doors disappeared, new ones appeared and you never knew where you were going to end up!

"You can use *this* bag if you like. It's one of my favorites!" the countess said, stroking a furry clutch bag that looked like a flattened mouse. Amelia wasn't sure she could fit her hand inside it, let alone a week's worth of

camping essentials. As Amelia tried to figure out a way to let her mother down gently, her dad appeared from the bathroom with a crossword puzzle tucked under one arm.

"Ah! My favorite sausage sizzler!" said Count Drake the Third when he saw Amelia. "You must be excited to escape organ practice for a whole week!" He winked mischievously.

Countess Frivoleeta glared at her husband. "Drake, my most dreadful flabbergaster, Amelia will be catching up with her organ practice after the half-moon break, won't you, darkling?"

Amelia sighed. "Yeess, Mom."

The Fang Mansion grimfather clock chimed, causing Amelia to shriek.

"It's already five a.m.! *I'm going to be late!*" she said, running along the corridor. "Where's my backpack?!"

Squashy bounced around in circles, waggling his stem and squeaking in shared panic.

"Do you mean *this* backpack, young Amelia?" came a familiar voice from the bottom of the stairs.

Wooo, the most respected ghost butler in the Kingdom of the Dark, floated up toward them, holding a round orange bag.

"Oh, Wooo!" said Amelia, running over to him. "You're the best!"

"I found it in the basement being cradled by a bogeyman. He'd adopted it as his pet." Wooo turned to the count and countess. "I'm afraid the bogeyman infestation is getting worse. We'll need to move them on quickly; otherwise they'll start to take over the whole house. They'll wear *all* your clothes, Countess, and then rip them up. *For fun.*"

Countess Frivoleeta looked as though she

might faint, and her left eyeball was spinning around so quickly it was dangerously close to falling out.

"It's okay, my dearest little pus-fart. We'll sort it." Count Drake nodded at Wooo and took a deep breath. "I'll call the Bogey Busters tonight."

With her pumpkin backpack filled to the brim, a few spare pairs of undies (JUST IN CASE) and a very bouncy Squashy, Amelia kissed her mom and dad goodbye. She was so nervous, her tummy felt full of fluttering vampire moths. She'd never been away from home for this long without her parents, not even when she ventured to Glitteropolis to find Tangine's mom.

Countess Frivoleeta straightened Amelia's

Rainbow Rangers sash. "I expect this will be FULL of badges by the time you return." The countess smiled. "You're going to have the *best* time."

"I hope so!" said Amelia. "I'll miss you and Dad, though."

"Oh, you'll forget all about missing us when you're having fun with your friends, my little toe-stopper," said Amelia's mom. "You won't want to come home!"

"And don't go eating anything you shouldn't," said Count Drake.

Amelia giggled. "Don't worry, Dad. I won't. A Rainbow Ranger must always be prepared. Plus, our Ranger leaders, Ricky and Graham, will be looking after us the whole time."

"Well, you take care, my little pimple-popper." Her dad smiled and gave Amelia a squeeze. He opened the vine-covered door that revealed a misty Central Nocturnia Graveyard.

"Right, then," said Amelia.
"My very first camping trip!
This is going to be the best half-
moon break ever!"

And with a wide-eyed Squashy tucked under
one arm, she stepped into the gloomy haze.

CHAPTER 2

PRINCE CAPTAIN

Amelia felt the spongy ground of the graveyard beneath her feet and breathed in the crisp night air. Squashy **pa-doing**ed around her ankles and bounced across to where a whole mishmash of excitable creatures were gathered, from zombies and yetis to ghosts, werewolves and serpents. At the front of the crowd were two large unicorns, each wearing a rainbow-colored scarf and a peaked cap with a rainbow logo sewn on the front.

"Galloping gaffer tape!" said one of the unicorns. "You see that tree there, Ricky?"

The unicorn named Ricky looked toward a blackened spiky tree. "Yeah, I see it, Graham. . . ."

"Well, don't you think it looks a little like me?" said Graham.

"Nah. I was thinking it looked much more like me, actually. Bit broader in the shoulders, good set of elbows . . ." Ricky paused, then added, "And bigger hooves."

"Well, it probably reminds both of you of, well, *both* of you," Amelia said as she approached. "It's the famous Petrified-Tree-That-Looks-Like-a-Unicorn."

Ricky and Graham looked at each other, then said at the same time, "Definitely looks more like me."

Amelia giggled at the two unicorns. She had already met Ricky and Graham, back when they were unicorn guards in Glitteropolis. Since then, Ricky and Graham had quit their guard duties, moved to Nocturnia and started the Rainbow Rangers club.

"Good to see you this fine half-moon break, Amelia Fang." Graham gave a dramatic bow as Amelia skipped backward out of the way of his very sharp unicorn horn.

"The half-moon break is my favorite time of year. Although this *is* the first time I've spent it away from home," said Amelia with a slightly nervous fang-filled smile.

"Be brave, little Creature of the Dark," said Ricky, wagging a reassuring hoof in Amelia's direction. "Rainbow Rangers look after each other, so you will be fine. And besides, me and Graham have got big plans for this trip. You'll have hardly any time at all to feel homesick!"

"Oh, I sure hope so . . . ," whispered a high-pitched voice from behind Amelia.

"Hi, Grimaldi!" Amelia hugged the little grim reaper, who had floated up beside her.

"I'm nervous too, but I am *so* excited to go camping together. No school for a whole week!"

"*And* no scraping small dead creatures off the streets!" Grimaldi added, waving his scythe around. "My grimpapa will have to take care of that while I'm away." Grimaldi Reaperton was a tiny reaper who dealt with the deaths of small creatures around Nocturnia. And even though Death was his middle name, he was actually scared of almost everything.

Suddenly, a CRASH was heard as the ground burst open a few feet away from Amelia and Grimaldi. The little reaper shot a mile into the air, and Squashy squeaked and bounced into Amelia's arms for comfort. A gravestone went hurtling past, followed by a very confused zombie head.

"My heeeeeeeeeeeead!" the head screeched as it rolled away into the woods.

Where the grave once stood, a huge yeti—NOT to be confused with a beast—appeared.

"IT'S THE HALF-MOON BREAK!" bellowed Florence Spudwick. "NO SCHOOOOOOL!"

"Hi, Florence!" replied Grimaldi and Amelia in unison.

Florence had been practicing her pit digging, a super-special yeti skill, every night. She had now mastered the art of digging her way around the city, creating her very own nifty network of underground tunnels—the latest of which ended right where the gravestone had once stood.

Prince Tangine La Floofle the First was the last of the Rainbow Rangers to arrive, accompanied by the loud PA-DOOFs of his genetically modified pet pumpkin, Pumpy.

"Sorry I'm late," Tangine said with a sigh. "I HAD to apply my eyelid cream and let it dry before I could leave."

Graham tapped his unicorn hooves impatiently and raised a skeptical eyebrow.

Prince Tangine was half fairy, half vampire, and lately rather fond of his nightly skin-care routine. He was also one of Amelia's best friends, along with Florence and Grimaldi.

"WHAT THE BATS ARE YOU PUTTING EYELID CREAM ON FOR?" said Florence.

"To prevent them from drooping," said Tangine with an air of superiority. "You'll be sorry when your eyelids get all droopy and I still look RAVISHING." Florence was just about to tell Tangine exactly what she thought of his eyelids when

Ricky the unicorn interrupted the excited chitchat of the group with an announcement.

"Good morning, Rainbow Rangers! Now that you're all here, I can finally tell you where we'll be camping for the half-moon break. We will be staying in a remote and quiet little place called Sugarplum Island. It's surrounded by the sea and is just a few miles east of the Kingdom of the Light."

There was a buzz of anticipation among the young Rainbow Rangers.

"Prepare yourselves for some awesome activities and the chance to earn a BUNCH of Rainbow Ranger BADGES," Ricky continued.

"Oooh! I LOVE badges!" squealed Amelia. She was determined to fill her Rainbow Ranger sash with as many badges as she could by the end of the half-moon break. Who didn't love a badge?!

"Whoever gets the most badges by the end of the week will be awarded the position of Rainbow Ranger Captain!" Graham added.

The Rainbow Rangers cheered and high-fived each other excitedly.

"That will be ME, of course," said a loud voice. Amelia, Florence and Grimaldi sighed. Frankie Steinburg was a ghoul in the same class as Amelia at school, and it was just typical that she would join the Rainbow Rangers too. She was very competitive and constantly trying to outdo everyone.

"Okay, Rangers!" Graham called over the commotion. "Before we leave, you know what to do. . . ."

Amelia and the rest of the Rainbow Rangers lined up. They straightened their sashes and saluted before earnestly reciting the Rainbow Ranger Promise:

"In the brightest day and the gloomiest night,
Whether I'm a creature of Dark or of Light.

I will be patient and grateful and kind,
And never leave a fellow Ranger behind.

I'll strive to keep learning. I'll trek and explore,
And promise to keep the Rainbow Ranger Law."

"I think I'm gonna cry," Ricky said, dabbing at his eyes with his rainbow scarf.

Graham was already sobbing. "Okay, Rainbow Rangers," he said through his sniffles. "Let's get this half-moon break adventure started!"

CHAPTER 3
THE OTHER LEFT

Amelia gazed through the Rainbow Wagon window as they trundled through the Kingdom of the Light, into the Meadow of Loveliness and past the Wishing Well of Well Wishes. Graham was driving and Ricky was giving directions.

"LEFT!" shouted Ricky suddenly, making everyone jump. "No, wait . . . THE OTHER LEFT. LIGHT. I mean, RIGHT. REFT?"

"Really, Ricky?!" Graham yelled as they narrowly missed a bewildered-looking pixie-hen in an apron. "You're HORRIBLE at this. Next time, YOU drive, and I'll read the map."

"Oh, we have a map?" Ricky asked.

"Yes, Ricky, you BIG ONION!" Graham said.

"Oh, NOW I've missed the next turn! This is all your fault."

As the Rainbow Wagon swerved and screeched through the Vivid Valley, Amelia was excited to see places in the Kingdom of the Light she'd never seen before, including the Marvelous Mountains, which glinted in their marvelousness, and the sweet-smelling Strawberry Streams. Although Amelia

and Grimaldi agreed that the smell of the dank, algae-covered river Styx was better.

Squashy was snoring lightly in Amelia's lap, and she began to feel her eyelids drooping. Back home she would usually be fast asleep at this time of the morning. But in the Kingdom of the Light, where the Rainbow Rangers were heading, things were the other way around. Amelia let out a big yawn.

After many winding roads and having scoffed too many sugary sweets, Grimaldi had managed to use every single sick bag available. He did not deal well with traveling for long periods of time. But finally, and much to everyone's relief, the Rainbow Wagon reached its destination—the Dazzling Docks. And boy, were they dazzling—the sea sparkled fiercely, making the Rainbow Rangers squint and shield their eyes as the shining waves lapped up onto the sandy beach.

"SO MUCH DAZZLE," Florence said, shielding her eyes as she stepped out onto the soft, sandy ground.

"Wow! I've never seen water like this before," Amelia said, staring at the sea. The bright shimmering waves washed away the last of her sleepiness. "It's so different from the Frogleg Falls or the Putrid Pond back home."

"It's definitely more sparkly," Grimaldi agreed, lifting a hand to cover his mouth. The brightness wasn't helping his travel sickness. "I think after a week of all these bright colors, I'll be relieved to go back home to the gray murkiness of Nocturnia."

The Dazzling Docks were packed full of little wooden boats all painted with different colors and patterns. Amelia liked the fact that each boat seemed to have its own personality. Ricky and Graham had gathered the Rainbow Rangers on the pier, where a huge sparkly

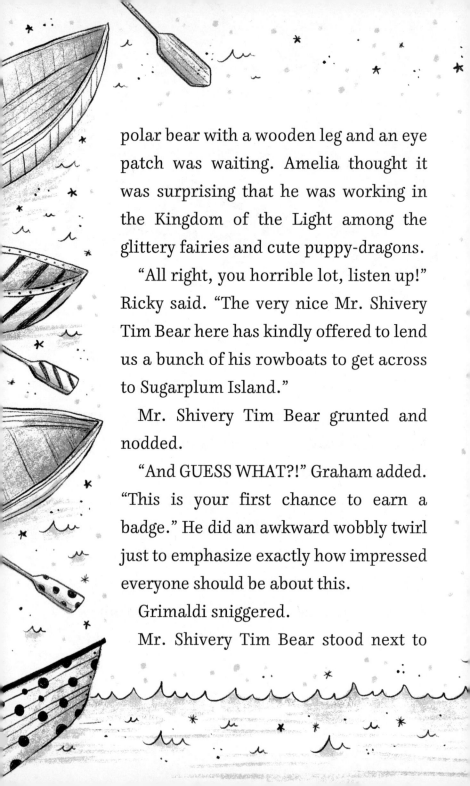

polar bear with a wooden leg and an eye patch was waiting. Amelia thought it was surprising that he was working in the Kingdom of the Light among the glittery fairies and cute puppy-dragons.

"All right, you horrible lot, listen up!" Ricky said. "The very nice Mr. Shivery Tim Bear here has kindly offered to lend us a bunch of his rowboats to get across to Sugarplum Island."

Mr. Shivery Tim Bear grunted and nodded.

"And GUESS WHAT?!" Graham added. "This is your first chance to earn a badge." He did an awkward wobbly twirl just to emphasize exactly how impressed everyone should be about this.

Grimaldi sniggered.

Mr. Shivery Tim Bear stood next to

Graham in silence. The polar bear didn't look very impressed.

"If you cross the water without sinking, you could earn your first badge! *But . . .*" Graham paused dramatically. "You won't just be rowing across to the island. . . ."

"Oof!" Amelia exclaimed as Frankie pushed in front of her, eager to hear how to win the badge.

"You will be racing!" Ricky declared, taking over from Graham. "The first Rainbow Ranger to reach the coast wins an *I GOT THERE FIRST* badge. So, in an orderly fashion, go and pick a vessel!"

Without hesitation, the Rainbow Rangers scrambled forward, desperate to find a boat and win the race.

Florence pushed her way through the

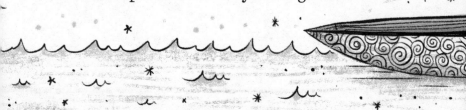

crowd and launched herself into a small polka-dotted boat. A huge wave rose in the air, soaking a shocked Ricky and Graham.

Amelia and Squashy made themselves comfortable in a black-and-white-striped boat, while Grimaldi found a swirly patterned one.

Tangine chose the most extravagantly decorated boat in the docks. It had four wrought-iron posts and lavish frilly red curtains. It resembled a floating canopy bed.

In the water next to Amelia was Frankie. Her narrow boat was covered in green spikes—

it looked a bit like a floating cactus. "Don't expect to beat me," Frankie said with a glare, getting ready for the race.

Amelia rolled her eyes and braced her oars.

"Good luck, Amelia," Grimaldi whispered from the boat next to her. "And make sure you don't let Frankie win!"

"Don't worry—I'll try my best!" Amelia said, smiling. She looked out toward Sugarplum Island as it glimmered on the horizon.

"Okay, Rangers!" Graham

shouted across the docks to the eagerly waiting racers. "Before you set off, there is one thing to be aware of—there have been rumors of shadows beneath the waves of the Sea of Sparkles . . . wiggles in the tides and secrets in the sea spray . . ."

"Graham, you're doing your annoying explaining-things-in-weird-ways-nobody-understands thing," Ricky said.

Graham sighed. "Fine. There's weird stuff in the sea, but no one knows what it is. *Okay?*"

The Rainbow Rangers muttered nervously among themselves, and Grimaldi peeked over the side of his swirly boat. Amelia leaned across and gave his hand a reassuring squeeze. "Whatever it is, it can't be as bad as what lives in the Putrid Pond or beneath the Nocturnian graveyard, right?"

Grimaldi giggled and nodded.

"You'll be fine!" Ricky assured everyone

with a big grin. "Just stay in your boat and everything will be grand." The Rainbow Rangers were silent.

Ricky cleared his throat. "All righty then! Let's get this show started. Ready, steady . . . ROW!"

Nobody moved.

Except Florence.

"OH, COME ON, WIMPITS! IT'S JUST A SILLY SEA STORY!" called a voice. It was their yeti classmate, who was already plowing through the waves using her own great paws instead of oars. "THAT BADGE IS MINE!"

At the word "badge," Frankie suddenly started rowing. "*I'm* totally getting the *I GOT THERE FIRST* badge!"

One by one, the Rainbow Rangers began to move away from the dock, and then, when nothing odd seemed to happen in the water below, they each sped up until a full-fledged race was on. Splashes and sploshes and shrieks of delight were heard as the Rainbow Rangers pulled themselves across the water.

"Come on, Grimaldi. Let's go!" Amelia called, setting off through the water as fast as she could row. But the little reaper was tucked away inside his boat, frozen to the spot.

"I . . . I'm worried about what's under there. . . ." He peeped over the side of his boat.

Amelia saw her fellow Rainbow Rangers rowing away across the water and felt that badge slipping away, too. "It's fine, Grimaldi!" she insisted. "Look, nothing is happening! Row next to me the whole way." She smiled encouragingly. "You can do it!"

Grimaldi hesitated, then pulled himself up into a seated position. He began to slowly move away from the dock.

"That's it—you've got this!" said Amelia.

"Now just move a *little* faster and we can beat Frankie!"

Grimaldi began to pick up speed, and soon the two friends were flying across the water to catch up with the rest of the Rangers.

Amelia rowed as fast as her little arms would go, with Grimaldi close behind. "I knew all those years of rowing along the river Styx with Grimpapa would pay off!" he called.

They giggled as they passed Tangine. Pumpy's end of the bed-boat was sinking in the water. They gradually overtook Rainbow

Ranger after Rainbow Ranger. As Florence was whizzing through the water just ahead, Amelia had a brilliant idea.

"Hey, Florence!" she yelled, slowing down a little, with Grimaldi following suit. "If me, you and Grimaldi tie, then maybe we'll *all* get the badge!"

"OOOH, GOOD THINKING, AMELIA!" said Florence. The three friends rowed side by side and made for Sugarplum Island. They were SO close now! Then . . . *BOMP!*

Something knocked the side of Amelia's boat, sending her wobbling off course. She shrieked as the little striped boat spun out of control.

"Oops! Sorry! Didn't see you there," Frankie said, smirking, and raced off in her spiky boat, passing Grimaldi and Florence, who had slowed down to make sure their friend was okay.

"WANT ME TO GO SIT ON FRANKIE?" Florence shouted.

"You guys just keep going, and I'll meet you at the island!" Amelia replied, waving them forward. "You still have a chance to beat Frankie! *Go, go, go!*"

She didn't mind being left behind just as long as Frankie *didn't* win.

Florence saluted; then she and Grimaldi raced ahead to try to catch Frankie as more and more Rainbow Rangers began to pass Amelia's boat.

Suddenly, Amelia felt something damp on her behind. When she looked down, she saw water oozing into her boat.

"Oh, no!" Amelia gasped. One of the spikes on Frankie's boat had made a big hole in the side of Amelia's little striped one. Squashy bounced into the growing puddle of water and tried to lick it up.

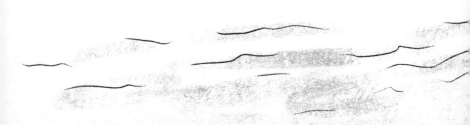

"It's okay, Squashy," Amelia said, picking the pumpkin up and hugging him to her chest. "I'm going to shout for help. Ricky and Graham will come and rescue us."

But just as Amelia was about to flag down the two unicorns, she felt a strong wind blowing the hair back from her face.

Her boat was moving.

CHAPTER 4

THE ISLAND IS YOUR PLATE

"How is this happening?" Amelia said, hugging Squashy tighter.

The little boat was heading straight for the shore of Sugarplum Island, overtaking all her fellow Rainbow Rangers, and Amelia wasn't doing a thing!

Amelia peered warily over the side of the boat, feeling slightly nervous about what she might see. Ricky and Graham had warned them about odd things lurking beneath the water—maybe they were right!

To Amelia's surprise, she couldn't see anything but her reflection and the bubbles from the waves the boat was making. Then Amelia thought she could *hear* something, a faint humming sound. She looked around, but everyone was too far behind her now for it to be any of her fellow Rainbow Rangers.

"Do you hear that, Squashy?" Amelia asked. She thought she was even beginning to make out a tune. Squashy certainly seemed to be waggling his stem from side to side in time with something. . . .

But before she knew what was happening, the boat somehow steered itself onto the sandy shore, and Amelia couldn't hear the humming anymore. She looked back at the water breathlessly, feeling utterly confused about what had just happened.

One by one, the other Rainbow Rangers began to pull up onto the shore next to her—including a red-faced Frankie Steinburg.

"You CHEATED!" Frankie snapped, storming up to Amelia's boat.

"Trust me, I really, *really* didn't," said Amelia, still feeling confused. "I didn't do anything!"

"You're LYING!" said Frankie, whose neck-bolt was spinning in anger.

"OH, BUZZ OFF," said Florence, stomping over and pushing Frankie out of the way. "WELL DONE, AMELIA! YOU'RE A ROWING CHAMPION!"

"You won the *I GOT THERE FIRST* badge!" Grimaldi cheered as he arrived in his little boat.

Amelia shook her head. "I . . . I . . . I didn't do anything!"

"DON'T BE SO MODEST!" Florence scooped Amelia up into a big hug. "YOU WON FAIR AND SQUARE."

The Rainbow Rangers gathered around Ricky and Graham as the two unicorns presented Amelia with her *I GOT THERE FIRST* badge.

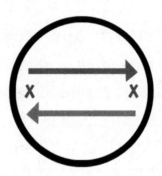

Frankie stood glaring at her, arms folded across her chest.

"Welcome to Sugarplum Island!" exclaimed Ricky. "We've got LOTS of exciting activities ahead of us this week. Graham has given each of you a special Rainbow Ranger guidebook, which has a map of the island and tells you exactly what you need to do to earn each

badge. You have the whole half-moon break to complete as many as you can."

Tangine was flicking through his guidebook, when he suddenly stopped and put his hand up shakily. "Um, excuse me, but this badge here says *FOOD FORAGING* badge?" He gulped. "As in searching for your food? As in . . . you *won't* be serving us a three-course meal every night?"

"EXACTLY!" Ricky and Graham said together, both looking very enthusiastic.

FOOD FORAGING
BADGE

HOW TO EARN YOUR BADGE

FIND ENOUGH EDIBLE SOURCES OF FOOD FROM YOUR NATURAL SURROUNDINGS TO SUSTAIN YOURSELF FOR ONE WEEK.

"You'll be learning to find your own food and prepare your own meals!" Ricky added. "That's how you'll earn your *FOOD FORAGING* badge. Sugarplum Island is filled with thousands of Bobbin-Berries, Frilly-Flowers and Dung-Pods of all shapes and sizes!"

"OOO, DUNG-PODS!" Florence said, licking her lips. "GONNA FIND ME A WHOLE BATCH OF THOSE!"

"We'll be eating off plates, though, right?" Tangine asked, looking a little wobbly. "China plates? With swirly patterns?"

Graham looked down at Tangine and lowered his glasses. "Oh, no, Tangine . . . The island *is* your plate."

Tangine held Amelia's shoulder for support. He took a deep breath. "Everything will be fine. At *least* I have my eyelid cream with me."

The Rainbow Rangers spent most of the afternoon setting up their tents and gathering kindling for a campfire.

As the sun began to set, everyone gathered around the fire to sing songs and toast Midnight Marshmallows.

Amelia kept admiring her *I GOT THERE FIRST* badge on her sash, but she couldn't help thinking she hadn't really earned it. Something else had helped her win the boat race, but she had no idea what it was.

Tangine sat on a log, studying the Sugarplum Island map. "So, do any creatures live on this island?" he asked. "And do any of them own a restaurant where I can get a nice cooked meal?"

"Ah . . . nobody has lived on this island for years," Graham said. "Only bizarre bugs and teeny-weeny creatures." He shuffled his log closer to the fire. "Years ago, many Creatures of the Light lived on the island. But gradually everyone left, and no one really knows why. . . ."

"They probably moved on before they got BORED to death . . . ," Tangine said, yawning. "Or starved from lack of quality waiter service."

"I like the idea of hunting for food that's REALLY nearby," a werewolf named Stink said, glaring at Tangine pointedly and licking his lips. "But for now, why don't we tell scary stories around the campfire?"

"Oooh, I have a story!" Graham said excitedly. "Who wants to hear my story?"

The young Rainbow Rangers nodded and the group got quiet.

Graham cleared his throat and began. "Once upon a time—"

"That's not how you should start a campfire story," Ricky interrupted.

"Oi! You just RUINED my moment," Graham huffed.

"Don't you know how a good campfire story works? You need to make it extra mysterious! Get the listener's attention right away," Ricky said, waving his hooves around dramatically. "It sounds like you're about to tell us a *love* story or something."

"No, it does not!" Graham said defensively. "I'll have you know it's a TRAGIC story. . . ."

"Bu—"

"ONCE upon a tiiiiime!" Graham sang so

loudly that Ricky's protests were completely drowned out. "There was a unicorn named Graham who realized he'd run out of TEA BAGS."

The Rainbow Rangers looked confused.

"Wait. *This* is your scary story?" Stink asked, scratching his hairy ears with a hind leg in disappointment.

"How else would you describe running out of tea bags?!" Graham said. "Imagine setting yourself up with your favorite mug and a plate of cookies, and then finding you can't make a cup of TEA!"

There was a long silence. One Rainbow Ranger had fallen asleep sitting up.

"*I* want to know what happens next!" said Amelia supportively. She felt bad for poor Graham.

Florence shot her a doubtful look.

Graham's eyes lit up. He sat up proudly and got ready to tell the rest of his story. But the Rainbow Rangers never got to find out what happened next, because at that moment, Gregory the goblin, who was sitting next to Frankie, sneezed loudly—and messily.

A HUGE globule of goblin snot flew into Frankie's face.

Frankie screamed, and Amelia and the other Rainbow Rangers looked on in horror as Bobbin the bat flew RIGHT through Sylvia the ghost's tummy in fright.

Sylvia was outraged. (You should NEVER pass through a ghost!)

And somehow, amid the chaos, Kevin the cyclops set fire to his behind.

CHAPTER 5

BEARDED BUGS

"Well, I guess that's story time over," Grimaldi said. Amelia picked up a bewildered Squashy, to keep him safe from the stampeding Rainbow Rangers.

Graham galloped past them, taking Kevin and his burnt bottom to the moonlit water.

"Well, I can't say I'm all that bothered about tea bags or boring Sugarplum Island," Tangine moaned. "I'm HUNGRY. I can't possibly wait for Kevin's rear end to be extinguished before eating. I'm going to go get some of the Royal Snacks that Mom packed for me."

Tangine opened his tent to reveal a very happy Pumpy munching through a jar of Revolting Brownie Bites. Every other jar that

once contained a Royal Snack was now empty.

"HEY! *Bad pumpkin!* You've eaten ALL my snacks!" Tangine snatched the tub away. He looked as if he might explode with anger. "You're out of control, Pumpy!"

From his safe spot in Amelia's arms, Squashy waggled his stem in amusement.

"WE COULD GO FORAGE FOR FOOD," said Florence, picking up a leaf and crunching it between her spiky teeth. "IT'S YUMMY! TASTES A LITTLE LIKE MOLDY SPLEEN," she added, wiping bits of leaf from the fur around her mouth.

Tangine huffed and walked farther into the trees. "Come on, Pumpy," he said, sticking his nose in the air. "Let's find a nice cheese and nostril baguette with extra toenail shavings."

"Tangine, I don't think we're allowed to wander off," Grimaldi said anxiously. "Plus, Ricky and Graham said that nobody lives

here anymore, so there won't be anywhere to buy food."

"I don't believe that. Ricky and Graham are just *saying* there's no one around so that we hunt for food on the GROUND. Well, I'm not doing that," declared Tangine. "There has to be a shop or a restaurant around here SOMEWHERE."

Amelia sighed and looked over toward the campfire. Stink the werewolf was howling at the half-moon, and Sylvia the ghost was flying in circles, wailing. Amelia's tummy rumbled, and she had to admit that Tangine had a point. Now that it was nighttime, she would usually be having her breakfast. "Let's at least tell Ricky and Graham that we're going for a walk," she said.

"Um, Ricky!" Amelia called over the chaos. But the two Rainbow Ranger leaders were busy trying to calm everyone down.

"Come on. Nobody is going to notice if we're gone for a bit," said Tangine. "My hunger is far more important than anything else. When I get too hungry, I shed unnatural amounts of glitter!"

"EWW!" said Florence as Tangine marched out of sight.

"We can't let him wander off alone," sighed Amelia. "Remember, *'Never leave a fellow Ranger behind.'* We'll just have to make sure we return before Ricky and Graham notice we're gone."

"Yeah, I don't want to get into trouble before the half-moon break has even started!" Grimaldi said, pulling at his hood nervously.

Amelia breathed in the warm night air as the friends trucked through a woodland made up of tall narrow trunks and an abundance of giant and exotic flowering plant life that they'd never seen in the Kingdom of the Dark. Everything was so pleasingly dead and rotten back home.

Florence assessed the forest floor for potential pit digging, and Grimaldi floated around the trees, around and around the trunks, over and under the branches. His scythe had a built-in torch, which was very handy for guiding the friends through the darkness.

Tangine had his Rainbow Ranger guidebook in his hand and was studying the map on the inside page. "I think we should head THIS way," he said, pointing ahead. "There's bound to be a nice place to eat at the top of the mountain."

"I AIN'T CLIMBING NO MOUNTAIN," said Florence.

"Fine," said Tangine, turning around, ready to stomp off. "I'll see you later, then."

"YOU'RE BEING A STUBBORN LUMP!" huffed Florence after him.

Suddenly, an orderly procession of bearded bugs flew past Florence's head.

"ARGH!" she bellowed. "I THINK ONE WENT IN MY EAR!" The little bugs scattered

as she flailed her wonderfully large and hairy arms.

Pumpy, quickly seizing the opportunity, PA-DOOFed up into the air and gobbled up one of the bugs.

"NO, PUMPY!" Tangine yelled. "STOP EATING ALL THE TIME!"

The bugs squealed and their little eyes turned bright green with indignation. They headed straight for Tangine.

"Uh-oh . . ." Tangine ran as fast as he could into the mountainous woods with the bugs close behind him. Seeing his trail of potential food flying away, Pumpy followed as fast as his heavy load could carry him.

"Tangiiiiine!" Amelia called. "Quick! We'd better run after him or we'll lose him!"

Amelia, Grimaldi, Florence and Squashy made their way through the woods as fast as they could. They jumped over mini-streams and shimmery flowers that occasionally erupted with little poofs of glitter.

"WHERE DID HE GO?!" Florence asked, wheezing.

Amelia was beginning to panic. Tangine was nowhere to be seen, and her legs were starting to ache as she ran up the impossibly tall and dark mountain. "TAAAANGIIIIINE?!" she yelled. *"Where are you?!"*

Higher and higher Amelia and her friends climbed and ran and stumbled and stepped, until suddenly the most unexpected sight stopped them in their tracks. . . .

CHAPTER 6

THAT GHOST PIE SANG TO THE PIGEON AT DAWN

"Wow!" Amelia gasped.

A ledge was carved out of the mountainside, and on it an incredible garden stretched before them. The whole scene was lit up by a beautiful tree.

"I've never seen a glowing tree before!" Grimaldi said.

Florence stomped over to the tree through the long grass. "IT'S FULL OF ROUND

THINGS. SOME KIND OF FRUIT OR SOMETHING. THAT'S WHAT'S GLOWING."

The tree was a sight to behold, with curly branches weaving their way around each other. From each branch dangled a plump yellow fruit, a bit like a Nocturnian Pus Plum, just less maggoty and stinky. They glowed a bright yellow-gold.

Pumpy was happily munching on some of the glowing plums that had dropped to the ground. Tangine was slumped on the grass next to him, catching his breath.

"The bugs flew away when we got here!" Tangine said, panting. "And look what I found! A tree with EDIBLE fruit." He reached up to a low-hanging branch and picked one of the golden plums. "Mmmmmmm . . . try one!" he said through a mouthful.

Florence picked one of the glowing yellow plums from a curly branch and took a nervous bite.

"GOBBLING GRUMBLE!" said Florence, taking another bite. "YOU'RE RIGHT. IT'S JUST LIKE BITING INTO A WONDERFULLY CONSTRUCTED YETI PIT!"

"That's not a taste," said Tangine.

"WELL, I CAN'T THINK WHAT IT TASTES LIKE . . . JUST SOMETHING REALLY, REALLY GOOD!" Florence said, picking another five plums and stuffing them all into her mouth at once.

"I feel like we should go back to camp now," Grimaldi said, looking around. "We weren't supposed to wander off this far. . . ."

"Grimaldi's right," Amelia said. She stroked her Rainbow Rangers sash thoughtfully. "But I guess this *could* count as foraging for food. . . ."

Her mind made up, Amelia reached

purposefully for a plum. It was velvety and light, and its gentle glow illuminated her pale skin. Amelia took a small bite and felt her mouth begin to water. The flavor was full and sweet and almost magical . . . like nothing she'd ever tasted before. She took another bite, and another.

All of a sudden, Amelia had forgotten about the urgency to get back to camp, and she was overwhelmed by the feeling of being very, *very* hungry.

"Thish ish delishush!" Amelia said through a mouthful. She picked another plum and held it out to Grimaldi. "Come on, Grimaldi. It's not going to bite!" She giggled. "We can record it in our Rainbow Ranger diaries to go toward our *FOOD FORAGING* badge!"

Grimaldi took it and cautiously bit into it. His eye sockets widened, and he smiled. "Wow! This *is* good. No wonder it's glowing!"

Florence stared at the night sky, looking content. "IT'S NICE HERE," she said.

"It is." Amelia yawned. She was beginning to feel unusually sleepy. "We should probably head back before we get too comfortable." The world around Amelia grew hazy and peaceful. She was aware that she needed to walk back to camp, but instead, she found herself lying down in the grass. She turned over and reached down to snuggle up with

Squashy, who had already begun lightly snoring at her feet.

"ANYONE ELSE REALLY WANT A NAP RIGHT NOW?" Florence asked. Then she gave an almighty yawn and slumped to the floor next to a snoring Tangine.

What's happening? Amelia thought sleepily. She felt Grimaldi curling up beside her.

"We should get back," he whispered. "Just five more minutes . . ."

"THAT GHOST PIE SANG TO THE PIGEON AT DAWN, DIDN'T IT?" said Florence. "WE SHOULD SEND HIM A LETTER. . . ."

"Yeah," Amelia agreed without thinking. "Wait . . . *What?*" she added as she slowly realized how little sense Florence was making. Her eyelids felt so heavy.

Maybe I should close them just for a second, she thought. They were still getting used to the time difference in the Kingdom of the Light, after all.

Amelia closed her eyes and fell asleep to the sounds of Tangine snoring, Florence's jumbled sleep conversations and shuffling footsteps in the distance.

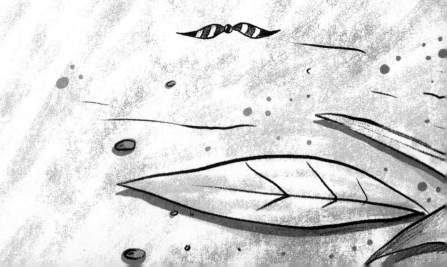

When Amelia woke, the full-moon was bright. She sat up and rubbed her eyes in confusion. The moon was meant to be a half-moon—it was the half-moon break, after all. . . . But as Amelia came to, she noticed even more moons.

Multiple moons?
What?

Amelia realized that the things she was staring at weren't actually full moons at all. They were the glowing plums on the tree. Except they were much, MUCH bigger than before.

Florence sleep-burped and woke herself up.

"YEESH," she said. "THEY'VE GROWN BIG."

Grimaldi yawned and rose slowly, followed by an annoyed Tangine.

"Where's my eyelid cream?" the prince mumbled. "I NEED my eyelid cream *right now*! Pumpy, did you eat it?"

Pumpy responded with one PA-DOOF and rolled over onto a sleepy Squashy.

Amelia looked around to see that the grass they'd been lying on had grown too. But not by a little—it was now three times as tall as Florence. And the Rainbow Ranger guidebooks that they'd been able to hold in one hand were now the size of tents.

"Hold on . . . ," Amelia started to say as the world around her began to make sense. She looked up and saw leaves as big as boats and flowers as big as houses.

"I don't think the plums are bigger," she said, feeling her stomach twist. "I think WE are much, *much* smaller. . . ."

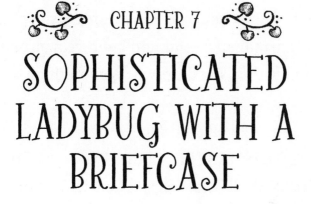

CHAPTER 7

SOPHISTICATED LADYBUG WITH A BRIEFCASE

"WE'VE BEEN SHRINKED!" Florence shrieked. "AAAAAAARGH!" She began panic-digging a tiny pit.

Grimaldi shakily held onto a blade of grass while Tangine stood with his hands on his hips, huffing and puffing. "Well, this just isn't good enough!"

"Okay, calm down, everyone," Amelia said, taking a few deep breaths. "It's all going to be fine." But Amelia secretly had no idea whether it was going to be okay or not. She didn't know

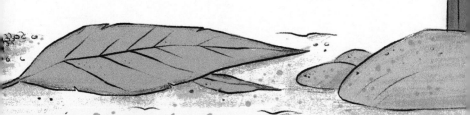

what else to say. Before she fell asleep, she was normal size, and had been very proud of the fact that she'd grown a whole inch since last year.

But now, well *now* she was the size of a—

"SOPHISTICATED LADYBUG WITH A BRIEFCASE!" Florence yelled from her tiny pit. And she was indeed pointing at a sophisticated-looking ladybug wearing a tie and carrying a large briefcase.

"*I say!*" said the ladybug in a deeper voice than Amelia had expected. "Did nobody tell you it's RUDE to point at a ladybug. Especially a sophisticated one." Then he walked off in a huff through the tall grass.

"Wait!" Amelia called after the ladybug. "Hello?! We need help! We're . . . Well, we're the wrong size!"

The ladybug reappeared with a frown. "What *are* you going on about?"

Amelia felt a little embarrassed. "Um, you see, sir, we're not usually this small. We're usually much, MUCH bigger."

"YEAH, LIKE WE-COULD-TREAD-ON-YOU KINDA SIZE," said Florence, her head poking out from her pit. The ladybug frowned harder.

"Don't listen to her," Tangine said, stepping forward. "Florence doesn't

know the meaning of sophistication like you and I." He leaned forward and whispered. "I don't suppose you have any spare eyelid cream in that briefcase of yours, do you?"

The ladybug raised his thick eyebrows. "And what are *you*? Some kind of moth?"

Tangine gasped and stroked one of his wings protectively. "How *dare* you!"

"Guys!" Amelia said urgently. "*The pumpkins!* Where are Squashy and Pumpy?"

"I haven't seen them yet," said a still-shaky Grimaldi.

The ladybug with the briefcase rolled his eyes and turned away. "You are very, VERY strange bugs and you are making me late for my dinner. So, goodbye!" and with that he walked away, grumbling a few grumpy words under his breath.

"RUDE!" said Florence.

"Come on, Tangine. We have to find our

pumpkins!" Amelia said, and swiftly ran off in no particular direction.

Amelia and Tangine weaved in and out of huge blades of grass, dodging pebbles the size of armchairs and Florence-sized loose plums.

"*SQUASHYYYYY! PUMPYYYYY!* WHERE ARE YOUUUU?!" Amelia yelled. "They could be ANYWHERE," she said to Tangine desperately.

Suddenly, Amelia heard a SNAP.

"What was that?" said Tangine.

Amelia looked around her, but there was nothing there. "It sounded like it came from above. . . ." And then the realization hit her. "Oh, no!" she cried.

It all happened so fast.

Amelia looked up to see a huge plum plummeting straight toward her and Tangine; getting closer and closer by the second. She

didn't have time to think before she was sent flying backward. Something solid hit her smack in the middle of her stomach, causing the air to leave her lungs as she hit the ground.

There was a loud THUD as the huge yellow plum crashed to the ground in the exact spot where Amelia and Tangine had been standing.

Amelia lay there in shock for a few seconds as she caught her breath; then she saw the familiar black eyes and cheery smile of her pet pumpkin peering down at her.

"SQUASHY!" she said, almost crying. Amelia scooped him up into a tight hug, never wanting to let go.

Tangine was still flat on his back, with a very proud-looking Pumpy sitting on his chest.

"Pumpy!" he wheezed. "I. Can't. Breathe."

Luckily, Pumpy spotted a mushroom nearby. He PA-DOOFed off Tangine's

chest, straight over to where it grew, and began nibbling at its giant stem.

Tangine sighed. "I will never be as good as food to that pumpkin," he said.

"AMELIA? TANGINE?" came Florence's voice. "WHERE ARE YOU?"

"Over heeeere!" Amelia called back.

Eventually Florence appeared through the grass, followed by Grimaldi, who was flinching

at every noise and plant he brushed past.

"AH, YOU FOUND 'EM!" Florence said, giving Squashy a tickle on the stem.

"Yeah, they actually saved us from a falling fruit," Amelia said. "We're going to have to be extra careful while we're so small."

"But we won't be staying this size forever—*will we*?" Grimaldi squeaked.

"Of course not," Amelia said. But she couldn't think exactly how they were going to get big again. She thought hard. "We were eating the fruit just before this all happened," she said suddenly. "Maybe it's something to do with that?"

"How on earth can eating fruit make you shrink? Eating it is supposed to make you GROW," Tangine said. "That's what Mom and Dad tell me, anyway."

The mention of the words "Mom and Dad" made Amelia's tummy feel all tight.

She missed her parents very much already, and the thought of not being able to get back to them made it a hundred times worse.

"What do we do now?" Grimaldi asked.

"Well," Amelia started. "Ricky and Graham are the grown-ups in charge, so we need to get back to camp and tell them what's happened. I'm sure they'll know what to do . . . ," she added sounding a little unsure.

"BUT IT'LL TAKE US FOREVER TO GET BACK TO CAMP," Florence said. "EVERY FOOTSTEP IS LIKE A MILE TO US NOW!"

A huge drop of water landed on Florence, soaking her fur from head to toe.

"EURGH!" she cried. "WHAT WAS THAT?!"

SPLOSH!

SPLOSH! SPLOSH! SPLOSH!

"I think it might be—" Amelia gasped as another **SPLOSH** of water hit her, almost knocking her over with the force of it. *"Raaaaaaain!"*

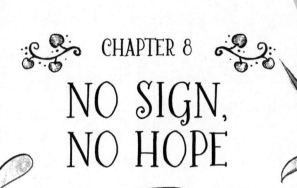

CHAPTER 8

NO SIGN, NO HOPE

Amelia picked Squashy up and held him tight. "The ground is going to turn into an ocean any minute!"

"Puddles are NOT as fun when you're this small!" shrieked Tangine, who was trying desperately to pick Pumpy up.

SPLOSH! SPLOSH! SPLOSH! SPLOSH! SPLOSH! SPLOSH!

The rain was getting heavier.

"Over here!" Grimaldi shouted from somewhere nearby. Amelia looked over and saw the little grim reaper floating toward them on a huge leaf.

Holding on to the pumpkins, Amelia, Tangine and Florence clambered on, trying their very hardest not to fall in.

"We've got to find shelter!" Amelia said, trying to protect Squashy from the rain with her stripy skirt.

"I GOT THIS!" Florence shouted, leaning forward. She put both of her strong arms into the water and began paddling hard. The leaf boat glided speedily along the water and through the garden.

The light coming from the glowing tree began to fade as they rowed farther away from it, and, apart from the torch on Grimaldi's scythe, the friends were soon in complete darkness.

But then, when it seemed like they couldn't get any wetter, it stopped. Amelia could still hear the sploshing of the rain behind them, so where were they? She squinted as her eyes started to get used to the lack of light. "Is everyone okay?"

"I'm not even thinking about the state of my hair from all that rain, but yes," Tangine said, patting his glittery head.

"I'M ALL RIGHT . . . ," Florence replied. "I THINK ONE OF THE PUMPKINS PEED ON ME, THOUGH. . . . I KNOW IT'S NOT RAIN 'CAUSE IT'S WARM."

Squashy blushed and wiggled his stem apologetically.

Amelia realized that she was able to see the outline of things around her. "Guys, I think we're in a cave!"

The friends fell silent as they took in the scene around them. The cave was full of beautiful paintings of the island propped up against the walls and lots of giant jars of yellow jam.

But that wasn't even the weirdest part.

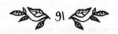

All over the cave walls, the days of the week had been scratched into the stone. And next to each day were the words "NO SIGN."

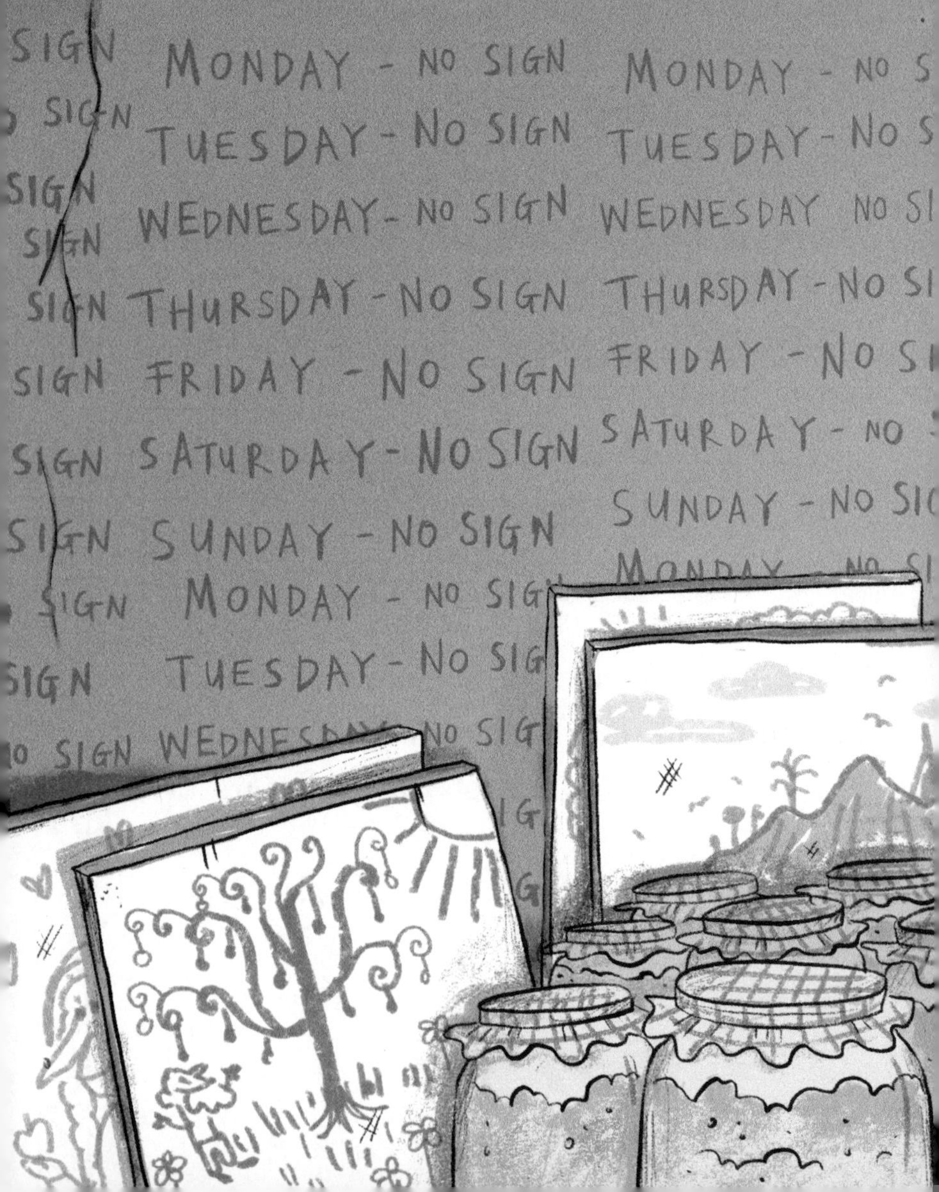

MONDAY - NO SIGN
TUESDAY - NO SIGN
WEDNESDAY - NO SIGN
THURSDAY - NO SIGN
FRIDAY - NO SIGN
SATURDAY - NO SIGN
SUNDAY - NO SIGN
MONDAY - NO SIGN
TUESDAY - NO SIGN
WEDNESDAY - NO SIGN

And then it started all over again. "I wonder what it means?" Amelia muttered, stepping out of the leaf boat.

"How odd," Grimaldi said, staring at the scribbled walls with big, wide, empty eyes.

"How TASTY!" said Tangine from somewhere else within the cave, followed by gobbling sounds.

Amelia looked up and saw Tangine leaning into one of the giant jam jars. He was scooping out handfuls of the yellow gloop and wolfing it down. *"Come taste this!"* he said through a mouthful.

"Tangine, I don't think you should do that. . . ."

But Tangine wasn't listening. He leaned

farther into the jar, eager to get more of the yellow jam. However, this time, it was too far—and he fell right in.

"Tangine!" Amelia gasped. She clambered up the jar as fast as she could and stretched an arm into it. "Grab my hand!" she said as Tangine flailed around in the sugary gloop.

Florence and Grimaldi came to help, holding Amelia by the waist so that she could lean her whole body in to reach Tangine. He was beginning to sink.

Pumpy bounced into the jar to try to save his owner, but his weight meant that he quickly sank to the bottom.

"PUMPY!" Tangine yelled, spraying a mouthful of jam.

There was a sudden BOMP, causing the jar to wobble. Florence and Grimaldi lost their footing and went tumbling with Amelia straight into the jar with Tangine and Pumpy.

95

Squashy pa-doinged around the outside of the jar in a panic.

"Don't bounce in!" Amelia yelled from inside the jar as Squashy poised himself to jump in. But her voice was muffled, and the little pumpkin was in a panic, desperate to get to her; with one big pa-doing he bounced into the jar.

The jam jar went tumbling to the ground, landing with a loud CRASH!

The friends went rolling in every direction across the ground.

"Oh, bothersome beetroot!" came a croaky voice from above. Amelia and her friends froze.

"A perfectly good jar of jam ruined!" said the voice. There was a shuffling sound and then a SWEEP, SWEEP, SWEEP and some humming.

96

"I know that tune," Amelia murmured. "But where from . . . ?" Before she had a chance to think about it, there was one big *SWEEEEEEEP,* and the gang found themselves—together with the broken remains of the jam jar, bits of cobweb, strands of coarse hair and a pile of toenail clippings— launched out of the cave, through the night air and into a patch of daisies.

CHAPTER 9
A CORN THAT BUMBLES

Outside, the rain had stopped, but the ground was still very wet and the puddles were the size of pools. Amelia squelched through the grass to check that Squashy was okay. He waggled a jam-covered stem at her reassuringly.

"I think Pumpy is still in the cave!" Tangine said in a panic.

"We'll find him, don't worry," Amelia said, although she didn't like the thought of going back into the cave to meet whoever or whatever had thrown them out.

The croaky voice suddenly rumbled out of

the cave again—"Out! Out! Pesky bugs!"—and something went hurtling through the air, landing with a THUD in the daisy patch next to them.

"PUMPY!" cried Tangine happily.

"What the bats just happened?" Grimaldi said, shaking the last of the dust from his cloak hood. "Who *was* that?"

Amelia's head felt fuzzy. "I don't know," she said. "But I do know that whoever it was didn't want us there. We need to get back to the campsite as fast as we can so Ricky and Graham can help us."

"What if we're stuck this size forever?" Grimaldi asked nervously.

Amelia didn't want to even think about that prospect.

"Don't be silly, Grimaldi," she said slightly more sternly than she meant to. "I'm sorry. I didn't mean to snap."

Florence put a big hairy arm around Amelia's shoulders. "COME ON, FANG. IT'S NOT LIKE YOU TO BE DOOM AND GLOOM. THAT'S GRIMALDI'S JOB!"

"Hey!" protested Grimaldi. Then he grinned. "It's true, though."

Amelia smiled. She could always count on her friends to cheer her up when she was feeling sad. She hugged Squashy tightly, and he nuzzled into her chest, when suddenly there was a low *buzzzzzzzzzzzzzzzzzzzz*. It quickly got louder. Amelia looked down at her friends in confusion.

"IT'S NOT ME," said Florence with a shrug.

There was a rustling sound from among the daisies. The buzzing stopped.

Amelia thought her cold vampire heart was going to beat right through her chest. *What's next?!* They hadn't even gotten far enough away from whatever was in the cave yet.

Grimaldi grabbed Amelia's arm, and Tangine hid himself behind Pumpy.

Florence stepped forward so that she was in front of Amelia, Grimaldi and Tangine, and poised herself, shaking down her fur in what she hoped was an intimidating manner.

The stems parted, and out flew a shocked-looking bumblebee.

"Oh, do pardon me!" the bee said, adjusting his little glasses. He was also wearing a crown and a cape and carrying a large staff with a glowing ball at the top. But that wasn't all. He had one long shiny and very pointy horn on his head. He held the staff out to get a better look at Florence. "Dancing dandelions. You're not a be—"

"THAT'S RIGHT," Florence bellowed. "I AM NOT A BEAST! I'M A RARE BREED OF YETI!"

Florence did not appreciate being mistaken for a beast. It happened sometimes, but she

was sure to let somebody know if they made that mistake.

The horned bumblebee took a step backward. "Oh, I do very much see that. What I was going to say was, you're not a *bee* . . . or any kind of bug, for that matter. Yet, you're the *same size* as one."

Florence narrowed her eyes. "YEAH . . . YOU'RE RIGHT."

"Please allow me to introduce myself. I am King Jamie the Eighth of Buggingtonshire," the bumblebee declared confidently. "And *I* am a bumblicorn."

"*A bumblicorn?*" Amelia said, peering out from behind Florence.

"Oh, hello!" The king laughed as, one by one, the others followed Amelia's lead. "Yes, the bumbliest of corns!"

"What? You're a corn that bumbles?" Tangine asked.

"No, no, I was just being silly with the words," King Jamie the Eighth explained. "I'm just a bumblicorn. . . ."

Tangine looked at him blankly.

"Goodness me," the king continued, buzzing over to Amelia. She instinctively stepped back.

"Oh, I didn't mean to startle you, young vampire creature," King Jamie said. "It's just, you seem to be hurt." He gestured toward her right wing, which had a big scratch across it.

Amelia lifted a hand to touch it. "*Ouch!* I must've scraped it when we fell out of the jam jar." Squashy squeaked and jumped into Amelia's arms to comfort her.

"You fell out of a jam jar?" King Jamie asked.

"THAT'S RIGHT," Florence replied. "HURT MY LEFT NOSTRIL."

"Flailing Flamingos!" King Jamie gasped, looking concerned. "You must be tended to!"

"I DUNNO IF I WANNA BE TENDED," Florence said, raising an eyebrow.

"Tended?" Grimaldi repeated. "Is that like being stretched?"

"Oh, no, dear little reaper," the king said kindly. "I think you're getting confused with *ex*-tended. I really think you should all come back to Buggington Palace so that we can tend to your wounds and find you some new clean and dry clothes too."

"Wait . . . did you say new clothes?"

Tangine asked, stepping forward. "My pride was hurt—does that count?"

"Thank you, King Jamie," Amelia said carefully. "But we really need to get back to our Rainbow Ranger leaders. They'll be worried sick when they realize we're gone."

"He *did* say new clothes!" Tangine said to Amelia. "I mean, look at the state of us! And yellow is *not* my color." He patted at the globules of yellow jam clinging to his vest.

"AND BEING THIS STICKY WOULD MAKE IT HARD TO GET VERY FAR RIGHT NOW," Florence said, lifting a foot, which left a trail of jam from her toes to the floor.

Grimaldi looked at Amelia nervously but didn't say anything.

Suddenly, something creaked in the darkness from the direction of the cave, followed by shuffling and footsteps.

"Okay!" Amelia said, deciding quickly. "We should get away from here, at least. . . ." She looked toward the cave anxiously. She didn't like the idea of being swept up again. "But as soon as we've cleaned up, we'll need to find Ricky and Graham so we can get back to our normal size!"

King Jamie saluted. "Follow me!"

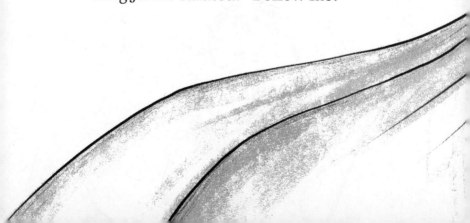

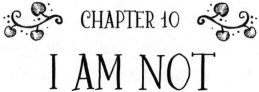

CHAPTER 10

I AM NOT A SOFA

As the friends followed King Jamie through the daisy patch, they answered all his questions about their half-moon break and what had led them to the tree. Soon, King Jamie took them up a little spiral staircase carved into a thick flower stem. Amelia hugged Squashy tight.

When the friends reached the top, the tall blades of grass and flowers parted to reveal a whole bug kingdom. All types of bugs were tucked away safely inside hundreds of colorful flower huts. The leaves on the flower stems

acted like little balconies where bugs had placed deck chairs and chaise longues. Vines, shoots and stalks connected each flower hut, acting as sheltered pathways. It was like nothing Amelia had ever seen before.

"Welcome to Buggingtonshire!" King Jamie said

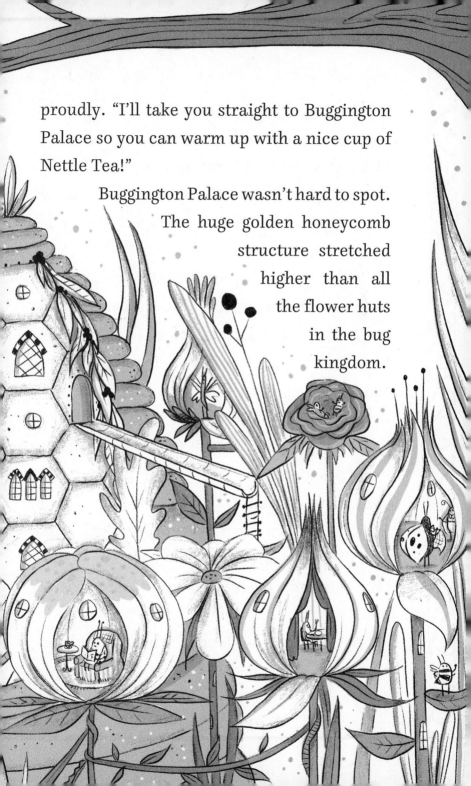

proudly. "I'll take you straight to Buggington Palace so you can warm up with a nice cup of Nettle Tea!"

Buggington Palace wasn't hard to spot. The huge golden honeycomb structure stretched higher than all the flower huts in the bug kingdom.

Inside, King Jamie the Eighth led the friends through spongy hallways lined with pictures of knights and past kings and queens. The air and walls were sweet with honey. Squashy leaned out of Amelia's arms to lick the walls as they walked past.

"Make yourself at home," King Jamie said, ushering the friends into a cozy living room lit by the warm orange glow from a huge fireplace. "I'll fetch you some dry clothes from the Honey Hall of Garments and have our wonderful maid, Madame Flutterby, make you a nice warm batch of Nettle Tea. Prickles or no prickles?"

Amelia smiled gratefully and hugged Squashy, whose eyes were now looking in two different directions from all the sugar. "Um, definitely no prickles for me, thank you."

"WAIT!" Tangine stepped forward. "Did you

say Honey Hall of Garments? As in a whole *hall* of clothes? Not just a wardrobe, or a room . . . a *hall*?"

"Indeed, Prince Tangerine," the king said.

"I WANNA PICK AN OUTFIT!" Florence shouted. "DO YOU HAVE CAPES?"

"A whole rack of them," King Jamie said.

Tangine beamed and Florence rubbed her paws together happily.

"Right this way, both of you!" said the king as he made to leave the room. "Amelia and Grimaldi, would you like to come and pick something to wear too?"

"No, thank you," Amelia said, feeling the crackling fire warming her toes. "The fire and some Nettle Tea should do the job."

"No problem," King Jamie started. Then he paused. "Oh! And you'll meet Denise in due course. . . ."

"Denise?" Grimaldi repeated as King Jamie

left with an excited Florence and Tangine behind him.

"No idea," Amelia replied with a shrug. She snuggled up with Squashy and Grimaldi on a big squishy sofa by the fire while Pumpy nibbled on an ornament.

"I think this is possibly the comfiest sofa I've ever sat on," Amelia said as she slowly began to sink into it. Grimaldi had sunk so far he had almost disappeared completely.

"Does it feel a little *sticky* to you?" he asked, looking slightly concerned.

Amelia shuffled and noticed her skirt slowly peel away from the surface of the sofa, leaving a trail of clear goo. "It can't be goblin slime," she said, poking at it. "Even goblins are too big for Buggingtonshire, aren't they?"

"It's like snot," said Grimaldi, wrinkling his nose.

"Sofa . . . sticky . . . goblin . . . *SNOT*?!" came a deep voice from somewhere in the room. "What do you plan on calling me next?!"

"Who said that?" Grimaldi asked, looking around.

Suddenly the sofa moved, and with one big *DOOOOING*, Amelia and Grimaldi were flung onto the floor.

"Ouch!" Amelia cried, rubbing her behind. Grimaldi had landed upside down in an elegant vase.

Two beady eyes blinked in the huge blue blob that Amelia had thought was a sofa, and then a long line appeared for a mouth. The eyes looked Amelia up and down. "I am NOT a sofa," it said coldly. "I am a rare breed of SLUG."

Amelia raised her eyebrows. "I think you're going to get along *very* well with our friend Florence."

CHAPTER 11

THE CURSE OF THE SUGARPLUM TREE

"BOW DOWN FOR THE MIGHTY FLO, YOU BIG LITTLE MITES!" Florence bellowed as she waltzed into the room where Amelia and Grimaldi were having tea with a massive slug.

Florence was wearing a long red velvet cape with a huge frilly collar and fur trim. A large golden crown was perched on her head, and she held a jewel-encrusted staff in one paw, which she used to point at whomever she spoke to. "DON'T I LOOK MAJESTIC?!" she asked proudly.

"Who's the beast?" the slug said before

taking a dainty sip of Nettle Tea with prickles.

Florence pointed her staff at the slug. "I AM NOT A BEAST. I'M A RARE BREED OF YETI!" She stepped forward and swished her cape for dramatic effect.

The slug gasped and bowed her head. "I immediately adore you. I'm Denise, by the way—a rare breed of slug."

Florence grunted and gently poked Denise in the tummy with the staff. "YOU'RE SO SQUISHY," she said. "PLEASURE TO MEET YOU. SO, WHAT MAKES YOU RARE?"

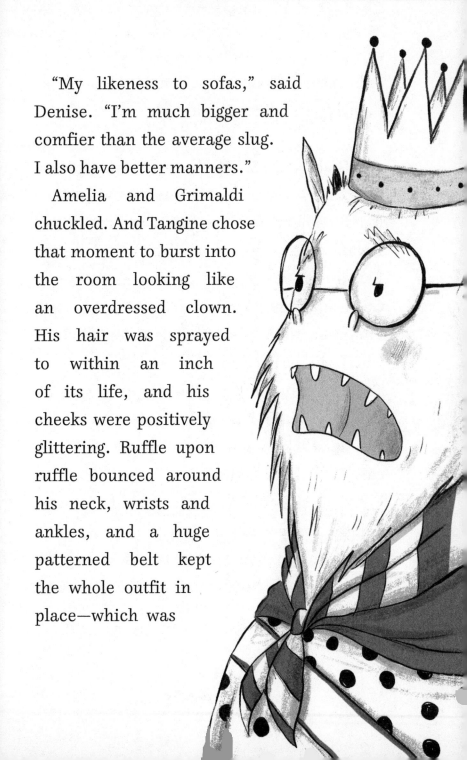

"My likeness to sofas," said Denise. "I'm much bigger and comfier than the average slug. I also have better manners."

Amelia and Grimaldi chuckled. And Tangine chose that moment to burst into the room looking like an overdressed clown. His hair was sprayed to within an inch of its life, and his cheeks were positively glittering. Ruffle upon ruffle bounced around his neck, wrists and ankles, and a huge patterned belt kept the whole outfit in place—which was not easy, considering Tangine looked as though he might explode right out of it with joy.

"LOOK AT ME!" He beamed and struck a pose. He walked up to Amelia and put his hands on her shoulders. "Amelia. I've decided I want to stay here and live in Buggington Palace. It's the *best*. I can be Bug Fashion Guru, and you guys can drink tea ALL DAY! Pumpy can live on a vegetarian diet of petals, which will be good for him. And Squashy . . ." Tangine paused and looked at the little pumpkin, who had fallen asleep with his tongue stuck to the honey-coated wall. "He can just lick the walls."

Amelia sighed. "We can't stay here forever, Tangine," she said softly. "We have to get big again and go home. Our families and our friends are in Nocturnia. I miss Mom and Dad and Wooo."

"Plus, we can't miss school. We have homework to hand in!" Grimaldi added.

"I DO MISS MY PIT," Florence said. "AND MY AUNT'S FAMOUS SLOW WORM SPAG BOL."

"I know," Tangine sighed. "I do miss Mom's selection of face masks and Dad's horrifying Hairball Hot-Pot, and my zombie Mummy Maids—especially Helen—it's just that I love that Honey Hall of Garments so much!" He slumped down on Denise.

"Seriously, I am NOT a sofa!" the slug cried.

"Well, when you're *King* of Nocturnia, you can open up your very own Hall of Garments!" Amelia said with a smile. "It can be your Horrifying Hall of Ghoulish Garments!"

Tangine's eyes lit up.

Amelia looked up at King Jamie. "I hope you don't think we're being rude. You're being so

kind, and your palace really is very lovely. It's just . . ." She paused and swallowed hard. "It's not home."

The king smiled. "I didn't think for one tiny second that you were being rude at all. I'm sorry you're in such a pickle."

"So, what exactly happened to you?" Denise asked.

"They ate the glowing fruit from *that* plum tree . . . ," King Jamie said, looking concerned.

Denise gasped. "Oh, the poor darlings have been cursed!"

King Jamie winced. "I didn't really want to mention that word. There's no need to alarm them."

"TOO LATE," Florence said.

"Cursed?!" Grimaldi shrieked. "We can't be cursed! Are we going to be tiny forever?"

Amelia felt her belly twist around and around. *Cursed?*

"It's what happened to everyone else on this island," Denise said sadly.

"I thought everyone left the island because it was so small and boring," Tangine said.

"Nobody ever *left* the island!" Denise exclaimed. "They're just all *teeny weeny*. All cursed! Like *you*."

"Over the years, the cursed creatures have adapted to being the size of bugs," King Jamie explained. "They've set up a tiny city called Miniopolis on the east side of the island. We trade honey with them once a year in return for their famous Nettle Tea."

"So what *is* this curse?" Amelia asked, not sure she wanted to hear the answer. "What happened exactly?"

"You've been touched by the Curse of the Sugarplum Tree, I'm afraid," the king said, turning to Denise. "Shall I tell the story? Or would you like to, my dearest sluggipops?"

"HOLD ON ONE MAJESTIC MINUTE," said Florence, pointing her staff at Denise. "ARE YOU TWO TOGETHER? LIKE *TOGETHER* TOGETHER?" She made the shape of a heart with her hairy paws.

The king laughed and shimmied up to Denise. "This is my wife, the queen of Buggingtonshire!"

"Oh, don't make a big thing out of it, bumblikins," Queen Denise said.

"Bothering Batwings," Grimaldi said, placing his head in his hands. "We're welcomed to the palace with open arms and the first thing we do is sit on the queen!"

The king and queen burst out laughing. "Don't worry about it, tiny death man," King Jamie the Eighth said. "I mistake my wife for a sofa more often than not!"

Amelia had thought Queen Denise was intimidating to begin with, but the more she got to know her, the more she liked her. Especially when she invited them to sit on her again while she told them the story of the Curse of the Sugarplum Tree. "I do take pride in how utterly comfortable I am, so JUST this once," the queen said, smiling as Amelia sank into her squishy exterior.

Queen Denise began. "Many, many, *many* years ago, an old gnome called Gretta Grubbikins and the love of her life,

a leprechaun called McJiggle, planted a sugarplum seed in their beautiful garden. Over the years, the seed and their love grew, until the most wondrous Sugarplum Tree blossomed. Gretta and McJiggle would dance and jig around the tree every day, humming their own very special tune together.

As the sugarplums grew, they would glow a most wonderful golden color. The pair shared the delicious plums from the tree with creatures from all over the island. And soon McJiggle even started sailing over to the Dazzling Docks every morning to sell them all over the Kingdom of the Light. The creatures LOVED them. Each night he would use the glow of the Sugarplum Tree to sail home safely to his beloved Gretta Grubbikins."

Florence sniffed. "THIS IS A LOVELY STORY SO FAR," she said, wiping an eye.

"BUT . . . ," Queen Denise continued.

"OH," Florence grunted. "I DON'T LIKE THE SOUND OF THAT *BUT*...."

CHAPTER 12

THE NECTAR CARRIAGE

"One night," Queen Denise started, "McJiggle did not return home. Gretta waited and waited, but morning came and still there was no sign of him."

"No sign . . . ," Amelia murmured to herself, remembering the scribbles covering the cave walls. "Wait! Was that *Gretta Grubbikins* inside the cave?"

King Jamie nodded. "Most probably. She's been hiding away in that cave for years now. She never comes out."

Denise nodded sadly. "So with every night that passed, Gretta grew lonelier. And as the years went by, the Sugarplum Tree was Gretta

Grubbikins's only reminder of her beloved McJiggle.

"And in her sadness, she no longer wished to share the sugarplums with anyone else until McJiggle came home. But the creatures of the island loved the fruit so much, they would still sneak into the garden to pick it.

"Before hiding herself away for good, Gretta cursed the tree. This curse meant that anyone who ate a sugarplum from the tree would shrink to the size of a sugarplum themselves. Then they would never be able to pick from the tree again.

"One by one, the creatures of the island seemed to disappear, and soon enough, Sugarplum Island appeared to be deserted."

"And that's the story of the Curse of the Sugarplum Tree," King Jamie the Eighth said, grimacing. "I'm sorry it's not better news for you all."

"I think that every day McJiggle didn't come back, Gretta Grubbikins recorded it on the walls of her cave," said Amelia.

"She lives in the hope that McJiggle will return," said Denise. "Wouldn't you, if someone you loved had disappeared?"

"Yes," Tangine said sadly. And Amelia realized that he was thinking of his own mom, who had been missing for years before Amelia, Tangine and the gang had rescued her from a unicorn prison. Amelia gave his hand a reassuring squeeze.

"If we can free your mom, Tangine, then we must be able to free ourselves from this curse, *somehow*!"

"There *must* be a way to break it," Grimaldi agreed hopefully. "All curses can be broken, right?"

"Well, yes, dear," said Queen Denise. "But I think the only way to break the curse would be

if McJiggle came back, and he was lost to the sea—lost forever."

"WELL, HOW ABOUT WE GO BACK TO THE CAVE AND TALK TO GRETTA?" said Florence. "TELL HER THAT CURSING ISN'T GONNA MAKE HER FEEL BETTER."

"I don't think it's quite that easy, fair yeti," said King Jamie kindly.

"Wait!" Amelia suddenly piped up. "Maybe, just maybe, we could *wish* ourselves big again at the Wishing Well of Well Wishes back in the Kingdom of the Light!"

"OOOH, THAT'S A GOOD IDEA, AMELIA!" Florence said, looking impressed. "I KNEW YOU'D COME UP WITH AN ANSWER—YOU ALWAYS DO." She smiled and put a big hairy arm around Amelia's shoulders.

"It's a strong curse," King Jamie said. "But a valiant idea and worth a try indeed!"

"We'll need to reach Ricky and Graham so

they can take us back to the Wishing Well. But I don't know how we're going to do that while we're this small," Amelia said, feeling very frustrated by it all.

"Where is your campsite?" King Jamie the Eighth asked.

"It's on the beach, facing the Dazzling Docks," Amelia replied.

"Ah, the west of the island," King Jamie said. "I can take you there in my special Nectar Carriage."

"Really? That would be amazing. You're being so kind to us, King Jamie," said Amelia. "Are you sure you don't mind?"

King Jamie smiled and stood up straight. "You are guests in my home. As king, I strive to do good for the community and help others. You are lost and in need of help, and I can do my very best to provide that help."

"Truth is, he loves ANY excuse to use his

139

shiny new Nectar Carriage!" Denise said, with one raised eyebrow.

Amelia giggled.

King Jamie gave his wife an affectionate nudge. "Is that what you think?" he asked. "That may be a *very* tiny part of it. But what's the point of a king who does nothing but sit on his throne and look pretty?"

"When I'm King of Nocturnia, I definitely plan to sit on my throne and look pretty," Tangine said, admiring his reflection in a long mirror on the wall.

"But if I can be even half the king you are, King Jamie, I'll know I'm doing something right."

King Jamie and Tangine bowed to one another.

"And I wouldn't mind a unicorn horn either," Tangine added.

CHAPTER 13

OI, KEVIN!

The sleigh-style carriage (made entirely of solid honeycomb) zipped through the air silently with Amelia and her friends tucked inside safe and sound. King Jamie sat on a small ledge at the front of the carriage, holding reins attached to a bustle of harnessed fireflies. Their bright glow lit the way through the night sky.

Pumpy was wriggling around on Tangine's lap, trying to catch the breeze in his mouth.

"May I ask that the big pumpkin be kept as still as possible, please?" King Jamie called back from the driver's seat. "We've never flown this fast before, and I don't want anyone to fall!"

Florence scooped Pumpy up with one paw and wedged him under her arm, much to the pumpkin's dismay. "HE'S NOT GOING ANYWHERE NOW."

As the flying carriage approached the west of the island, tiny beacons of light became visible from around the Rainbow Ranger campsite. The lights were moving, heading toward the sea. As the Nectar Carriage drew closer, Amelia noticed the Rainbow Rangers, including Ricky and Graham, holding flashlights and climbing into their boats.

"Wait a minute," said Amelia, feeling like a brick had fallen into her stomach. "They're leaving!"

"What?!" Grimaldi shrieked. "They can't leave! Ricky and Graham will be gone, and we'll have no way of getting big again. We'll be stuck here forever!"

"We need to hurry!" Amelia said, feeling panic wash over her.

"Which of those creatures are Ricky and Graham?" King Jamie asked.

"THOSE BIG UNICORNS THERE!" said Florence, pointing toward them.

"Okay, hold on tight!" King Jamie yelled. *"FASTER!"* he commanded the fireflies, guiding them downward at top speed.

Everything appeared to blur as the carriage whizzed through the air faster and faster, making Amelia's eyes water. The fireflies' wings were flapping so quickly, it looked as if they weren't moving at all. Then, close to the ground, just as they had almost reached Ricky and Graham, a high-pitched SQUEEEEEEEEEEEEEEEAK was heard.

One of the fireflies floundered in midair and the Nectar Carriage swerved, spinning high into the air as the frantic insects reared off course.

Amelia gasped as King Jamie went tumbling to the sand below.

Florence clambered to the front of the carriage and grabbed the reins.

"Can anyone see King Jamie?" Amelia cried, leaning as far over the side as she dared.

Her head spun as she looked down from

high up. But sure enough, there on the sand, with his crown knocked off, lay the royal bumblicorn.

Just a few yards away, the Rainbow Rangers were pushing their boats into the water, and for a moment, Amelia didn't know what to do. If they went back to help King Jamie, the boats would be gone—and the gang would have lost their chance to get home.

But really there was no choice.

"We have to go back and make sure that King Jamie is okay!" Amelia said, climbing into the seat next to Florence and taking one of the reins.

"But I don't *want* to be small forever!" Tangine protested from the back.

"Tangine . . . King Jamie helped us," Amelia gently reminded her friend. "We have to help him!"

Tangine nodded, looking a little bit ashamed.

"BAAAAAACK!" Florence bellowed at the fireflies as she and Amelia pulled tightly on the reins—and away from the Rainbow Rangers.

When they landed, they found King Jamie with his legs up in the air and his bumblicorn horn stuck in the sand.

"Is . . . is he dead?" Grimaldi asked nervously.

"No." King Jamie the Eighth opened his eyes slowly and weakly waved up at the concerned faces above him. "But you must go! Fly on, young Nocturnian friends!"

"THANK THE GRAVE!" Florence cried. "LET'S GO!"

But when Amelia and her friends looked up, all they could see were the silhouettes of little boats bobbing away toward the horizon.

It was too late.

They were in a very sticky situation indeed. And this time it had nothing to do with jam.

"They've gone." Grimaldi's little voice broke through the shocked silence.

Amelia couldn't speak. She clutched Squashy tightly to her chest as tears dripped down her face.

"I am so sorry," King Jamie said. "I shall renounce my crown straightaway and give it to that young one-eyed man over there."

Florence sighed sadly. "NO, YOU DON'T HAVE TO DO THAT, KING JAM—" She stopped. "ER, WHAT? WHAT *YOUNG MAN*?"

Everyone looked up to see Kevin the Cyclops running toward the shore, dragging a small boat behind him. "Wait for meeeeee!"

Amelia jumped into action. "King Jamie, can we borrow your carriage to fly over to that cyclops, please?"

"Of course!" the royal bumblicorn replied, looking very relieved. "And may all the luck of Buggintonshire be with you!"

The Nectar Carriage veered up toward Kevin, their very last hope of being big again.

The cyclops climbed into the boat, and Amelia shouted as loud as she could, "KEVIN! *HEY, KEVIN!* IT'S ME, AMELIA, AND EVERYONE ELSE! WE'RE HERE!"

But Kevin couldn't hear her. He picked up his oars.

The carriage drew closer.

Kevin seemed to sense something near his head and sat up a little straighter.

"OI, KEVIN!" Florence yelled. She had a much louder voice than Amelia.

"He can't hear us!" Amelia shouted. "We need to get in front of his eye!"

Florence managed to steer the Nectar Carriage back around to face Kevin.

"KEVIIIIIIIIIN!" they shouted again as they flew toward his face to get his attention. Everyone waved their arms.

Kevin's one eye twitched. He put down an oar and slowly lifted a hand in the air. He must have recognized them!

"ARGH! BLASTED BUGS!" His hand swatted the carriage away.

The Nectar Carriage went crashing toward the Sea of Sparkles. The fireflies scattered and flew away in different directions.

Amelia saw King Jamie flying nearby. He tried to reach out and grab her and her friends, but they were just out of reach.

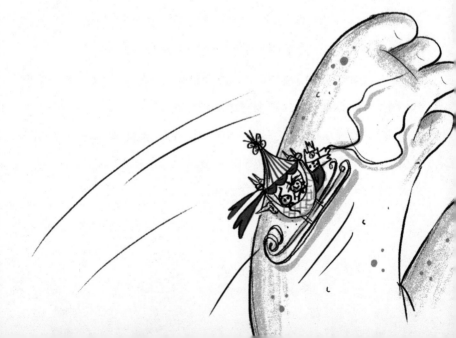

The stars in the sky disappeared from her view. King Jamie was but a distant buzz, and the last thing she saw was the flickering glow of the fireflies as she sank deeper and deeper into the water.

CHAPTER 14
CORAL JUICE

"You okay, honey?"

Amelia felt something nudge her shoulder softly.

She slowly opened her eyes. She felt dizzy.

"Easy does it, lovely one," said a voice.

Amelia was lying on something soft and kind of fluffy. As she yawned, a big bubble of water rose from her mouth. She felt as if she was moving in slow motion. Everything seemed wibbly wobbly, like she was underwater.

And then, as everything came into focus, she realized . . . she *was* underwater!

"Thank the oysters you're okay!" said the voice again.

Amelia looked to her side to see a friendly-looking creature with caramel skin; short, squiggly white hair and big eyes staring straight at her.

"I'm Nurse Bubble!" the creature said. "How are you feeling, Amelia?"

Amelia winced as she sat up a bit too fast, her wing still hurting. "Where am I? Where are my friends? And Squashy? Is he okay?"

Nurse Bubble placed a hand gently on Amelia's shoulder. "It's okay, your friends are well, tucked up nice and cozy too, here in the Oyster Infirmary in the Kingdom of Aquatica! Grimaldi, Florence the rare fluffy one and Prince Tangine are all together! And your little pumpkin and his large pumpkin friend are busy munching on a bowl of Kelp Krispies."

Amelia took a deep breath. Her thoughts slowly unjumbled, and she remembered what had happened. Her heart sank—because of her decision, they had missed the boat. She knew they had done the right thing saving King Jamie, but she couldn't believe they weren't on their way to the Wishing Well of Well Wishes.

Amelia leaned back against the pillow and looked around. Everything around her was spectacular. Clusters of colorful sea plants of all shapes and sizes swayed lightly in the current, and small creatures with tails, fins and googly eyes swam in and out of them.

Stretching as far as the eye could see were bobbly huts covered in brightly colored lichen and pretty flowers. Curly weedlike plants weaved themselves around pebbles, and every so often, bursts of rainbow bubbles would erupt from pointy rocks.

"It's pretty, isn't it?" the nurse said, swishing her glimmering yellow fishtail. She gave a big friendly smile, revealing two big vampire fangs.

Amelia gasped.

"Why, you look a little alarmed," Nurse Bubble said as she turned around and plumped up Amelia's pillow. "Ooooh, of course! You've probably never seen a mer-pire before, have

you? But look!" Nurse Bubble clapped her hands. "Here are your friends to see you! I would prepare yourself a little, Amelia Fang!"

"Why do I—?" But Amelia stopped midsentence, staring in amazement as a star-shaped Squashy, with suckers on each of his five-pointed arms, came bobbing through the water to her bed.

He was followed by Grimaldi, who had a wispy black fishtail.

Pumpy soon appeared, munching on something red. He had a big curly seahorse tail. It was a very strange sight indeed.

Nurse Bubble rushed over and removed the red thing from his mouth. It turned out it wasn't food at all—it was another nurse who happened to be a very anxious-looking crab.

"Sorry about that, Brenda," said Nurse Bubble as Brenda huffed and scurried away.

"I THINK I LOOK QUITE GOOD WITH A TAIL!" bellowed Florence, swimming in and

swishing her big fluffy tail in circles, creating a mini whirlpool.

"At least you GOT a tail!" said a familiar voice. Tangine swam over. "Do NOT laugh." He folded his arms and frowned. Instead of a fishtail, Tangine had eight long tentacles. "These do NOT suit my complexion!"

Amelia giggled while fixing her blankets. That was when she saw it. Instead of a pair of legs, she had a fishtail.

"Gaaaaaaaaaaah!"

"Coral Juice!" the mer-pire nurse gently ordered a shocked Amelia, brandishing a flask in her face. "It'll make you feel much better. And, you know, it's what gave you all the ability to swim and breathe underwater!"

Suddenly a jolly voice boomed, *"Nurse Bubble!* My ol' whipper-snapper! I hear we've some new patients in need of my silliness."

"Our new patients are awake and are certainly in need of your love and care!" Nurse Bubble said, giving a small and old mer-creature a big hug.

"Aye, jolly good, jolly good," he replied. He was very wrinkly, with a long white beard and long hair. He had a green glittery fishtail and wore an apron that was covered in paint splatters. His face was a kind one, with rosy cheeks and a mischievous smile. "I'm Mr. Grubs, resident artist, entertainer, smile-maker and General Takerer-Carerer of the injured. I'm here to make you laugh and help heal those wounds." He did a little jig and spun on the spot.

Nurse Bubble introduced the friends to Mr. Grubs. "This is Amelia, Florence, Grimaldi and Tangine."

Tangine tried to hold out a royal tentacle to be greeted by Mr. Grubs but ended up in one big knot.

"They're creatures from the Land Above. Took a terrible fall about an hour ago," said the nurse.

An hour ago?! thought Amelia. Ricky, Graham and the Rainbow Rangers would definitely be back in the Kingdom of the Light by now—probably on their way back to Nocturnia. How would they ever get back now?

"You look sad, Amelia. What's wrong?" Nurse Bubble asked gently.

Amelia turned to her uncomfortably. "It's just, um, I'm sorry, Nurse Bubble. But we really need to get back home to reverse a curse—we need to get ourselves big again. I just don't know how we're going to do it. . . ."

The others all looked worried too. Tangine gave Florence's hairy hand a reassuring

squeeze, and Squashy gave Amelia's fishtail a comforting lick.

"A curse, you say?" Nurse Bubble's already huge eyes widened, and she glanced at Mr. Grubs quickly, before shaking her head as if dismissing a thought. "Well, that does explain why you were the size of my hand when I found you. The trusty Coral Juice made you bigger," she said.

"That stuff's a doozy!" Mr. Grubs chuckled.

"Wait," Grimaldi said, the big black holes of his eyes as big as Nurse Bubble's. "Does that mean we're *not* tiny anymore? And the curse is broken?"

Amelia felt an ounce of hope explode inside her chest, and Florence snorted in shock.

"Oh, honey, I'm sorry," Nurse Bubble said. "I'm afraid not. You'll return to your tiny size the minute you're back on dry land. The Coral Juice only works underwater."

Amelia sighed and watched as a huge manta-ray dragon floated past the window, making a low, rumbling *WAAAAAAAAAAA-AAAOOOOOOOOOOOOOOOOAAAAAAAA* sound.

"We do appreciate you saving our lives, Nurse Bubble. But we really need to go now." Amelia tried to get up and swim, but Nurse Bubble put a hand gently on her shoulder and guided her back into the shell bed.

"I think you should rest up a bit before you go anywhere," said Nurse Bubble with concern. "You have a few bumps and bruises. And it's the middle of the night, so you'll need your sleep. Myself and Mr. Grubs here will make you feel right at home."

"It's okay, we're not tired," said Amelia, easing herself out of the shell bed.

"Well, that's the perfect excuse for some painting, then! A nice bit of art is one of the

best ways to relax! I'll go fetch my paints and some paper!" said Mr. Grubs, swimming off and humming to himself.

Amelia gasped. "It's that tune again!"

CHAPTER 15

THE TIDDLYPIPS WING

Florence, Tangine and Grimaldi piled onto Amelia's shell bed with Squashy and Pumpy pa-doinging and PA-DOOFing behind them. "THIS PLACE IS CRAZY," Florence said. "I KNOW WE NEED TO GET HOME SOON, BUT I NEVER THOUGHT I'D SEE THE DAY WHEN I'D GET TURNED INTO A MER-YETI!"

"I bet nobody's seen mer-death before!" Grimaldi giggled.

But Amelia was too distracted by what she'd just heard to think of anything else. "Guys! I heard that tune again! I heard it when I was being pushed along in the boat and won the race, and it's the same tune Gretta Grubbikins was humming in the cave."

"Maybe it's just a popular song that creatures sing around here," Grimaldi said.

"Maybe . . . ," said Amelia. "I don't know. But I can't help feeling like it means something more."

"WHADDYA MEAN?" Florence asked, looking doubtful.

"I've just been wondering *how* someone who lives under the sea would be humming the *exact* same tune as someone who hides away in a cave."

Nurse Bubble swam merrily into the room to refill their flasks of Coral Juice.

"Nurse Bubble," Amelia started. "Who exactly *is* Mr. Grubs?"

"Why, he's the loveliest merma-chaun in the Kingdom of Aquatica!" she said, beaming.

"He did admire my brand-new tentacles,"

Tangine agreed, waving one around grandly.

Grimaldi giggled.

"But was he *born* here?" Amelia asked, as Squashy snuggled into the shell next to her.

"No . . . ," said Nurse Bubble, smiling at Amelia curiously. "He's from the Land Above. My mother was working here at the Oyster Infirmary many years ago when they found him. He was unconscious and had a massive bump on his head, and when he eventually woke up, he couldn't remember anything about, well, *anything*! Since he couldn't even remember his name, he decided to call himself *Mr. Grubs*! It was the first thing that popped into his head."

Nurse Bubble sat Amelia up gently and straightened her covers. "He's such a lovely man—when I was a little mer-pire, I used to visit Mr. Grubs while my mother worked long shifts, and he'd tell me jokes and paint me

wonderful pictures, always humming his little song."

Amelia could feel Nurse Bubble's fondness for Mr. Grubs as if it were a big warm blanket of love.

"Do you know," Nurse Bubbles continued, "that whenever he's not helping around the hospital, he's at the water's surface helping anyone crossing the water from here to Sugarplum Island."

Suddenly Amelia remembered how her little boat seemingly sailed itself across the Sea of Sparkles. *It must have been Mr. Grubs!*

That was when she'd first heard him humming that tune. But what kept him going back and forth from here to Sugarplum Island?

"Is there something on your mind, little vampire?" Nurse Bubble asked Amelia, tipping her head to one side.

But before Amelia could ask anything, she was stopped by the sound of Tangine calling urgently.

"Ameeeeeeeelia!"

Where was he? Amelia hadn't even realized he'd left the room.

"Tangine?" she called. "Are you okay?"

A few tentacles poked out from the open doorway, gesturing for Amelia to follow.

"He must be in the Tiddlypips Wing," said Nurse Bubble, looking slightly confused. "That's where the baby sea creatures sleep, so best keep it *hush-hush*!"

"GET OUT OF THE BABY ROOM, YOU BIG NUT," Florence said, swimming over to collect Tangine by the tentacle. Then she stopped. "OH, BUT SPEAKING OF NUTS . . ."

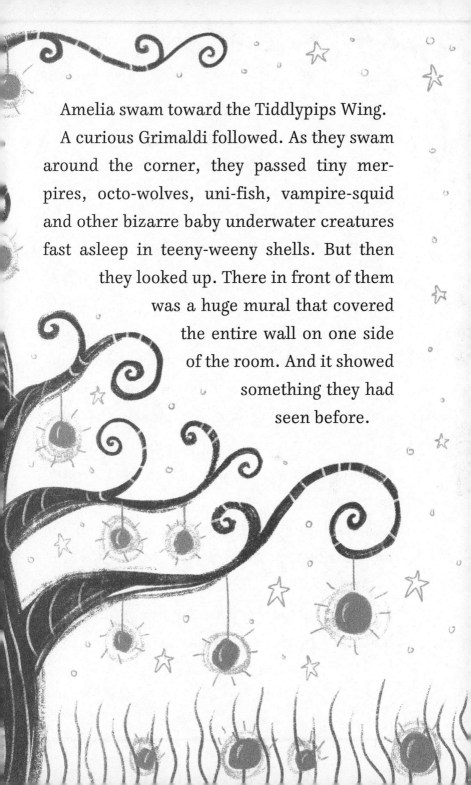

Amelia swam toward the Tiddlypips Wing.
A curious Grimaldi followed. As they swam
around the corner, they passed tiny mer-
pires, octo-wolves, uni-fish, vampire-squid
and other bizarre baby underwater creatures
fast asleep in teeny-weeny shells. But then
they looked up. There in front of them
was a huge mural that covered
the entire wall on one side
of the room. And it showed
something they had
seen before.

"It's the Sugarplum Tree," Amelia said quietly. "The only thing the gnome, Gretta *Grub*bikins, had left of her beloved leprechaun, McJiggle, before he went missing, sailing plums to the mainland."

"MR. GRUBS!" Nurse Bubble cried. "I think you might have something there, little vampire!"

Amelia nodded excitedly.

"*What?!* I demand to know what everyone is wondering. And why haven't they told me, when I am the prince and clearly the most important person here?" Tangine huffed, waving his many tentacles around indignantly.

Grimaldi's eyes widened as it dawned on him too. "Grubbikins . . . Grubs . . . Mr. *Grubs* . . ."

"McJIGGLE!" Florence bellowed, then quickly put her hands over her mouth as a baby mer-pire stirred in the corner.

"Creeping corals!" Nurse Bubble whispered in excitement. "Can it be we *finally* know where Mr. Grubs came from?"

Amelia grinned, feeling like a light inside her had pinged on.

"Hold on," said Tangine as the penny finally dropped. "Now, let's say Mr. Grubs *is* McJiggle, Gretta's one true love. Well, if it's anything like all the Kingdom of the Light fairy-tale books I've read, then maybe, just maybe—"

"OH MY FLIPPERS, GET ON WITH IT!" Florence groaned.

Tangine shot her a glare, then flourished his tentacles. "What I was saying before I was rudely interrupted was MAYBE True Love's Kiss could break the curse! *Our* curse!"

"I AIN'T KISSING NO ONE," Florence said folding her arms.

"Ummm . . . I don't think he meant you," Grimaldi added.

177

"Yes, Tangine!" Amelia cried. For the first time since they'd been at the Oyster Infirmary, she felt much, much better. She twirled around in the water. "If we reunite Gretta with McJiggle, then surely she'll lift the curse and we can be big again!"

CHAPTER 16

IT'S ALL COMING BACK TO HIM!

That familiar tune filled the Oyster Infirmary, and Mr. Grubs came swimming into the main room with his arms full to the brim with art materials.

Amelia poked her head out from the entrance of the Tiddlypips Wing.

"Whatchy'all doing in there?" said Mr. Grubs as he laid out some paper. "I've got some arty treats here for you!"

"That tune you were humming . . . ," said Amelia, approaching Mr. Grubs as her friends swam in behind her. She felt oddly nervous

and was glad they were all there together. "I think I've heard it somewhere before."

Mr. Grubs looked at Amelia and lowered his glasses. "Really?" he asked, furrowing his brows. "How does a wee girl like you know a funny tune like that, then? It's always in my head. Not sure where it came from."

"That's just it," said Amelia. "I think I *may* know where it comes from. I'm not one hundred percent sure, but it's possible . . . well, if my feeling is right . . ."

"We might have figured out who you really are!" Nurse Bubble said, rushing over.

Mr. Grubs took his glasses off. "Bubble dear, you've been working a long shift. Perhaps it's break time?"

Nurse Bubble took his hands gently. "No, Mr. Grubs. The tree you painted in the Tiddlypips Wing . . . well, Amelia and her friends say they've seen that tree before.

On Sugarplum Island—in the Land Above."

"Sugarplum Island?" Mr. Grubs repeated, raising an eyebrow.

"There's a gnome that lives there," Amelia said. "Years ago, a leprechaun she loved very much disappeared. His name was McJiggle, and her name is Gretta Grubbikins."

Mr. Grubs stared at Amelia for a second, then plopped down on the edge of one of the shell beds.

"Gretta Grubbikins . . . ," he muttered under his breath, as if he was searching in the depths of his mind. "I feel like I know that name." Mr. Grubs put a hand to his chest. "But I'm afraid I can't remember. I'm sorry." He bowed his head in sadness.

The friends floated in silence.

"Maybe he's not McJiggle after all," Grimaldi said quietly.

But then Amelia started humming a tune.

The same tune she'd heard when her little boat was pushed along the water. The same tune Gretta had hummed in the cave. The same tune Mr. Grubs had been humming earlier.

Mr. Grubs looked at her. He began to hum along. Then he closed his eyes and stopped humming and whispered gently. "Gretta. My beloved Gretta Grubbikins." His eyes began to well up. "It's all coming back to me!"

"IT'S ALL COMING BACK TO HIM!" said Florence, waving her tail around and slapping Grimaldi smack in the middle of the eyes. A baby bat-fish began to cry.

"And I am McJiggle Grubbikins!" the merm-achaun declared delightedly. He rose and danced a little jig, surrounding himself in small bubbles. "I remember who I am! I am McJiggle, and I live on Sugarplum Island with my beloved Gretta!"

"Oh, thank the grave," Tangine said,

adjusting his knotted tentacles. "Maybe *you* can tell her to stop cursing everyone."

"What do you mean?" McJiggle asked, looking a little confused.

Amelia blushed. "Hmmm . . . well, the thing is, Gretta was so upset about losing you that she cursed the tree so anyone who eats from it shrinks to the size of a sugarplum. The tree is her only reminder of you, and she didn't want anyone touching it after you'd gone."

McJiggle looked a little embarrassed. "Oh, well, that's no good at all!"

"Oh, honey! Isn't that lovely?" Bubble said, spinning on the spot. "To have someone love you so much, they're willing to CURSE others to keep the memory of you alive!"

McJiggle sighed and took Bubble's hands in his. "My dear, dear Bubble. You have shown me nothing but love and kindness all the years I've lived here. I don't know how to thank you."

Nurse Bubble hugged him tight. "Mr. Gr— I mean, *McJiggle*. Actually, you'll always be Mr. Grubs to me." She smiled. "I truly am delighted that you remember who you really are. You don't need to thank me at all. You have been a dear friend to me since I was a tiny mer-pire, and even though I'm going to miss you more than you'll ever know, you will never, ever be forgotten here."

McJiggle chuckled. "Just don't miss me so much that you put a crazy curse on anyone, eh?"

Amelia and her friends looked at each other, unsure

how to react. Then they all burst out laughing.

"GROUP HUUUUG!" yelled Florence, and dragged everyone into her furry embrace.

"Well, I guess you should head to the shore," said Nurse Bubble once she'd reluctantly stepped back from the wonderful yeti hug. "You need to get back to your Gretta!"

"Well, this is goodbye," said Nurse Bubble a few minutes later. "Once you set foot—or should I say, *fin*—on land, the Coral Juice will wear off. You'll soon have your normal bodies and return to the tiny size you were before."

Amelia sighed. She'd gotten used to being big again—even if she did have a tail!

"It's okay." McJiggle grinned. "You'll be in good hands," he said, holding out his own. "I'm

sure there'll be enough room on my ol' wrinkly palms to carry you lot when we're back on shore."

"Oh, definitely," Nurse Bubble chuckled. "They were teeny-weeny and super cute when I found them."

"Well, that goes without saying," said Tangine, fluttering his eyelids.

Nurse Bubble smiled. Amelia, Florence, Grimaldi and Tangine all gave her one last hug goodbye, then she gave Squashy and Pumpy some extra Kelp Krispies to munch on.

McJiggle was last to say farewell.

"At least I know I'll be in good hands if I ever have a boating mishap again." He winked. "I will never forget what you have done for me."

Nurse Bubble took a deep breath. "Well, I've decided to rename the Oyster Infirmary,"

she said with a grin. "If you ever find yourself toppling into the sea again, you might well end up in the Jigglygrubs Infirmary."

The friends burst out laughing.

Nurse Bubble gave a little twirl and waved. "Goodbye my friends from the Land Above!" And she disappeared into the depths of the Sea of Sparkles.

CHAPTER 17
THE TINGLE

The sun shone brightly on the horizon as Amelia opened her eyes. Her clothes were wet, and a now GIANT McJiggle was sprawled out on the sand next to her. She'd almost forgotten how small the curse had made them. Squashy and Pumpy were rolling around in a pile of crispy purple seaweed nearby.

"My hair is an utter MESS!" Tangine said, sitting a little farther away and trying to pat down the glittery frizz. "Whoever said sea salt was good for texture was SO WRONG."

McJiggle stretched his legs out. "Shuddering sugarplums," he said. "I haven't used these in years!" He wiggled his toes. "Amelia? Amelia's friends, whose names escape me? I know

there was a fluffy one and one with wings . . .
and a small deathly one. Where are you?"

"McJiggle!" Amelia called as loudly as
possible in her tiny voice.

The old leprechaun looked around,
confused.

"Down here!" Amelia yelled, waving her
arms. "Guys, I need your help getting his
attention. He can't hear us!"

"*Wooooooooooooo, McJiggle! Over here!*"
cried Grimaldi.

"*Hellooooooooo!*" Tangine called.

Florence climbed up to McJiggle's ear. "YO!
JOLLYJIGGLES!" she bellowed. This seemed
to do the trick.

"Oh, my!" said McJiggle, turning his head
from where he lay and spotting a tiny Amelia,
Florence, Grimaldi and Tangine. "You
mentioned the curse made you small, but
I didn't realize *how* small!"

"YEAH, YOU CAN THANK GRETTA FOR THAT," said Florence.

"Ah my apologies, dark creatures of Nocturnia." McJiggle scooped the little friends up in his wrinkly hands.

"COME ON THEN, McDOOGLE," Florence said. "LET'S GET YOU HOME SO WE CAN BREAK THIS CURSE!"

Amelia looked up at McJiggle. "Are you ready?" she said softly.

He closed his eyes and took in a deep breath. Then he opened his eyes and looked toward the top of the mountain. "I'm coming home, Gretta."

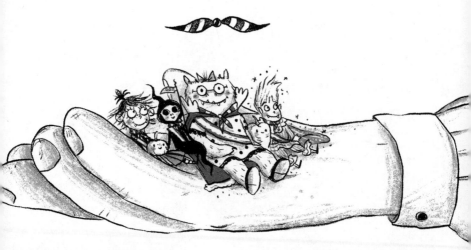

The Sugarplum Tree was still glowing, even in the morning sunlight.

McJiggle stood at the edge of the garden holding Amelia, Florence, Grimaldi, Tangine and the pumpkins safely in his hands.

"I . . . ," he began, then gulped. "I don't know what to say. It's been so long. What if Gretta doesn't recognize me or thinks I'm too old and wrinkly now?"

"DON'T WORRY, McJIGGUMS. I'M SURE GRETTA'S GOT A FEW WRINKLES HERSELF," Florence said.

"I can recommend a great eyelid cream," Tangine suggested.

Florence elbowed him. "NO ONE'S INTERESTED IN YOUR SILLY EYELID CREAM," she said.

Amelia stood up and looked McJiggle in the eyes. "Of course Gretta will recognize you! She loves you!"

"Enough to curse an island," Grimaldi said with a nod.

"If you're not sure what to say, why don't you hum?" Amelia suggested.

McJiggle smiled. "I think that's a wonderful idea," he said, placing Amelia and her friends down carefully on a low branch of the Sugarplum Tree. "Wish me luck," he said, and then sat down beneath the tree, closed his eyes and began to hum his and Gretta's tune. Squashy waggled his stem in time with the tune, and a light breeze caused a few sugarplums to fall to the ground.

But there was no sign of Gretta. Amelia held on to Grimaldi's hand tightly.

"Why isn't she coming?" Grimaldi asked.

McJiggle looked over at Amelia. He looked

heartbroken. Amelia began to feel hopeless.

But then McJiggle hummed again, this time louder and with passion. He stood up and started to walk toward the cave as the tune resonated through the leaves. Even the sugarplums seemed to glow a bit brighter.

And that was when Amelia felt Florence bump her shoulder. "HEADS UP!" she said.

Amelia looked up and saw movement in the cave entrance at the end of the garden. McJiggle walked toward the cave, humming all the time— and soon, instead of one voice, there were two, as Gretta Grubbikins emerged from the darkness of her cave for the first time in years.

She walked across the garden slowly, using a wooden stick to support her. She stopped in front of McJiggle.

"It can't be . . . ," Gretta breathed.

"My Gretta," McJiggle whispered as he took her hand in his.

Tangine sniffed.

"AWW, YOU ALL EMOTIONAL, TANGINE?" Florence said, putting a big hairy arm around Tangine's shoulders.

"No!" said Tangine defensively, wiping his eyes. "YOU'RE emotional."

"Does anyone feel a bit tingly?" Grimaldi asked, scratching his arms.

"I waited for you every day and every night," Gretta said to McJiggle. "I didn't want to believe you were gone. But after years of waiting, I'd lost hope. I never thought I'd ever see you again!"

And with that, Gretta hugged McJiggle so tightly, it looked as though she might squeeze the life right out of him.

"OKAY, I FEEL THAT NOW," said Florence, wincing. She shuffled and wriggled. "MOVE UP, TANGINE!"

"I can't!" Tangine snapped. "Your huge

behind is in the way! Hey, Amelia, can't you move up?"

"There's no room!" she said as Grimaldi squealed. "I'm going to fall off! Stop pushing!"

And then there was a SNAP as the branch gave way beneath them.

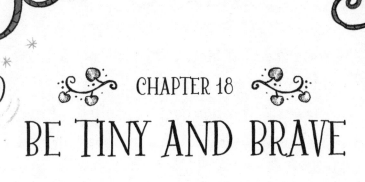

CHAPTER 18

BE TINY AND BRAVE

Amelia, Florence, Tangine, Grimaldi and the pumpkins fell to the ground. Amelia braced herself for a very sore behind but soon realized they hadn't actually fallen very far.

They were normal size once again!

McJiggle, still hugging Gretta, gasped.

"The curse has been broken!" Amelia yelled.

"AND SO HAVE OUR BACKS!" Florence moaned.

Gretta gazed at McJiggle. "I swore the curse would break if you came back to me."

"Ah, yes." The leprechaun smiled. "I hear you've made quite an impact on this island. . . ."

Gretta blushed. "They were picking our plums!" Then she softened. "I'm sorry. All I had left of you was the Sugarplum Tree."

"IT'S ALL RIGHT," Florence cut in. "GUESS WITHOUT THE CURSE, WE WOULD NEVER HAVE FOUND McJIGGLY, EH?"

Gretta giggled. "I don't know how to thank you for bringing my McJiggle back," she said sincerely.

"Maybe by NOT sweeping us up and chucking us out into the rain?" said Tangine.

"Tangine!" Amelia hissed, putting her head in her hands.

Gretta's eyes widened. "Oh deary dear," she said. "My eyes aren't too great these days. I did think it was a little odd when that jam jar fell over and smashed!"

Everybody laughed before the sound of hooves and rustling was heard in some nearby trees. Suddenly, two flustered-looking unicorns appeared.

"Ricky, Graham!" said Amelia, running over to them. "We thought you'd left!"

"Galloping gooseberries!" Ricky said as Amelia threw her arms around him. "Thank the stars you're safe! We'd all sailed around to the other side of the island to find you when some king corn-bum-number-eight—"

"He's a *bum-bleeee-corn*, actually," Graham corrected him.

Ricky frowned. "Yes, that's what he said. Anyway, the king baggicorn came along with a WHOLE kingdom's worth of bugs and surrounded us!"

"Ricky thought they were gonna attack us," said Graham, rolling his eyes.

"You thought it too! And STOP interrupting my story!" Ricky added defensively. "But anyway, it was only to get our attention, and he told us what had happened—that you'd fallen into the sea! We were beside ourselves! Jamie the bumbaborn guided us here to find a gnome named Gretta who'd done a curse or something."

"You said it wrong again, Ricky," Graham said. "King Jamie is a bumpy-corn!"

"Bumblicorn," said a very small but familiar voice. "But you can just call me King Jamie. And it's really not worth squabbling over."

The Nectar Carriage bobbed up and down in the air. Queen Denise was sitting in the back, fanning herself. "Coo-eee!" she called happily.

"KING JAMIE!" Amelia and her friends shouted in unison.

"I'm so glad you're okay," he said. "What happened?"

"Don't worry!" said Amelia with a grin. "We were taken care of by a mer-pire called Nurse Bubble—there's a whole other kingdom under the Sea of Sparkles!"

"Really? I never knew about that!" said the bumblicorn.

"It's where we found McJiggle! He's been living under the sea all this time," said Amelia.

The king gasped. "And THAT'S why you're big again! And you're not the only ones. The curse has been broken! There are creatures all over the island popping up out of nowhere. They've all returned to their normal size!"

Frankie came running through the trees, shouting, "AMEEEEEELIA! Where are you? I'm sorry for always being such a SNOOT. *Ameeeeelia? Amelia's frieeeeends? Prince Booooy?*"

When she appeared and saw Amelia standing next to Ricky and Graham, she stopped in her tracks. "Phew!" She smiled with relief. "I mean, WHERE have you been?! Running off so that WE have to go on a wild-gooseberry chase looking for you ALL night!" she harrumphed. Then she added quietly, "I'm glad you're okay, though. It's boring when there's no one to compete with for badges and grades."

Amelia grinned. The rest of the Rainbow Rangers gradually appeared, covered in twigs and mud and various bugs.

The last to make his way to the scene was Kevin, who looked very uncomfortable.

"I am SO sorry," he said. "Um, I didn't

realize the thing buzzing around my face last night was you."

"In a weird and twisted way, you helped us," Amelia said kindly. "If it wasn't for you, we wouldn't have fallen into the water and found McJiggle, and then reunited him with Gretta Grubbikins over there."

McJiggle gave a friendly wave. "Well, isn't this grand! Has anyone had breakfast yet?" he called over the chitter-chatter.

The young creatures mumbled and shook their heads. Amelia gave her rumbling tummy a rub. She hadn't realized how hungry she was after their long night of adventuring.

"I hear there's some delicious fruits in these parts," McJiggle said as he picked a handful of sugarplums from the tree. "C'mon, there's plenty here for everyone!"

Amelia, Florence, Grimaldi and Tangine looked a little awkward. "Um . . . are they *safe* to eat now?" Grimaldi said.

Gretta and McJiggle laughed. "Why, yes, of course!" Gretta said. "The curse is broken!"

"The only curse these plums are responsible for now is the curse of being FAR TOO DELICIOUS!" McJiggle said, taking a bite.

And soon all the Rainbow Rangers were picking plums from the tree and gobbling them down.

After a whole day of munching sugarplums and dancing around the Sugarplum Tree, Ricky and Graham took the Rainbow Rangers back to the campsite.

McJiggle and Gretta joined them to share stories around the campfire. Kevin sat farthest away from the fire. McJiggle told the tales of his time under the sea, while the Rainbow Rangers roasted Midnight Marshmallows and dipped them in Gretta's famous Sugarplum Jam.

"Ricky," Graham said. "We should have made a *BROKE A CURSE* badge, shouldn't we?"

"Well, it's not really your everyday activity, is it?" Ricky said.

"But they broke a whole curse," Graham said. "That's pretty big."

Ricky and Graham eventually decided to present Amelia and her friends with three brand-new badges that they made from bits of scrap paper and leaves: the *BROKE A CURSE* badge, the *BE TINY AND BRAVE* badge and the *FIND A LOST LEPRECHAUN* badge.

Amelia, Florence, Grimaldi and Tangine had all the Rainbow Rangers listening in awe as they retold their adventures of the previous night. Tangine took it upon himself to act out the whole story.

"I think we should raise a sugarplum to Nurse Bubble," McJiggle said.

"TO NURSE BUBBLE!" the group cheered.

"And also to my new friends, Amelia, Florence, Grimaldi and Tangine. For bringing me home!"

"TO AMELIA! TO FLORENCE! TO GRIMALDI! TO TANGINE!" cheered the Rainbow Rangers.

"And to Gretta," Amelia added.

"FOR CURSING US?" Florence asked.

213

"Well, what I was *going* to say was . . . to Gretta," Amelia said. "For a future full of happiness, love and many, many sugarplums!"

CHAPTER 19

ONE SMALL BEACON OF LIGHT

During the rest of the half-moon break, Amelia's sash filled up with badges. She earned the *FOOD FORAGING* badge, the *HOP UP THE MOUNTAIN* badge and, with King Jamie's help, she achieved the *BOMBASTIC BUGS* badge.

Florence was the only one to get the *FOOD THAT FARTS* badge, and every Rainbow Ranger got a *BUILD A SUMMERHOUSE FOR RICKY AND GRAHAM* badge.

By the end of the week, Amelia felt like she'd learned a lot and found she hadn't thought about being homesick once. While

she still missed her mom and dad, she was having so much fun with her friends—and as long as she had them, she was home.

Frankie Steinburg ended up as the Rainbow Ranger Captain, much to Tangine's disappointment, but Amelia didn't mind. It didn't matter how many badges she had, because she had achieved something far bigger and better. She had played a part in bringing together two creatures who had been apart for years and finally lifting the Curse of the Sugarplum Tree.

The gang did, however, each receive a special *SEA OF SPARKLES* badge, hand-painted by McJiggle himself. Creatures of the Light who had once been cursed and now returned to their normal size cheered on Amelia and her friends as McJiggle presented them with their new badges. Gretta even promised Tangine that she would build a shiny new restaurant on the island to remember them by.

"May I request you call it the Tangenius Temple of Tantalizing Treats?" Tangine asked. At which the crowd burst out laughing, and Gretta accepted his request, then gave him a great big hug.

"I'm going to be sad to leave this place," said Grimaldi as the Rainbow Rangers packed their bags.

A BUZZZZZZZZZZZZZZZZZZZZZZZZZZZ echoed through the air as King Jamie flew down to join Amelia and her friends. He and Queen Denise had visited them every day over the week and brought tiny sacks of honey especially for Squashy.

"It was such a pleasure to meet you all!" King Jamie said.

"I'll miss your Hall of Garments," Tangine said sadly. He still wore his frilly outfit with pride.

"DENISE," Florence said. "YOU'RE THE RAREST BREED OF SLUG I'VE EVER HAD THE PLEASURE OF TALKING TO."

"And you
are definitely
NOT a beast."
Denise smiled.

Grimaldi bowed. "Thank
you for helping us, King
Jamie," he said shyly.

"You were very brave," the bumblicorn
said. "If you were a bug, I'd have you as one of
my loyal knights!"

Grimaldi went all silly and blushed.

"Amelia Fang," King Jamie the Eighth started to say, "you and your friends will always be welcome to visit us in Buggingtonshire!"

Amelia giggled. "We might be a little bit big," she said. "But of course we will!"

"Just as long as you don't try to sit on me again," Denise said. "Especially now!"

"What a week!" Amelia sat happily in her little stripy boat with Squashy right next to her. This time, Grimaldi joined her at the opposite end, as his swirly boat was being used to transport all the jam Gretta had given to the Rainbow Rangers as a goodbye gift. The other Rainbow Rangers were all gathered together, ready to sail back to the Dazzling Docks. "I can't wait to tell Mom and Dad all about it . . .

although, they probably wouldn't believe the part where we got cursed and were the size of bugs AND then hung around in an underwater kingdom with fishtails. . . . Tangine looked so funny with those tentacles, didn't he?"

But Grimaldi was curled up at the end of the boat, snoring lightly. Amelia didn't blame him. It had been a very eventful half-moon break.

Amelia rowed and rowed across the Sea of Sparkles as the sun began to set in the sky, marking the end of the half-moon break. She looked down at her sash full of badges and smiled. She would cherish it forever.

Amelia's arms began to grow tired. She was so close to the Dazzling Docks . . . but then, as she shifted the heavy oars in her hands, they slipped into the water with a *PLOP PLOP*.

"Oh, pottering pumpkins!" she said, trying to reach them, but the oars were floating away.

Just as Amelia was about to shout for Ricky

and Graham, she felt the boat begin to move forward faster and faster until it was almost flying along the water. Clinging to the side of the boat, she peered over the edge and thought she saw a glimpse of squiggly white hair.

Amelia let the warm evening breeze brush over her until the boat sailed into the Dazzling Docks.

Grimaldi woke up and stretched. "Oh, we're back already?" he said, looking a little embarrassed. "Sorry. I didn't mean to fall asleep. Thanks for rowing us all the way, Amelia."

Amelia raised her eyebrows and smiled. "I didn't do a thing."

As she stepped out of the boat and lifted her pumpkin backpack, she looked out to the Sea of Sparkles and whispered, "Thank you, Nurse Bubble."

On the horizon was Sugarplum Island, now filled with creatures, as it had been all those years ago. The sun had almost set, casting a deep purply-red shadow on the island, but on its peak was one small beacon of light—the glow of the Sugarplum Tree.

After the best break she had ever had, Amelia felt braver than ever before. She smiled as she watched the Sugarplum Tree glow in the distance, and thought of the two creatures who would be dancing around that tree every morning and every night, for as long as they lived.

THE END

RICKY AND GRAHAM'S

RAINBOW RANGERS

BADGE HANDBOOK

I GOT THERE FIRST
BADGE

HOW TO EARN YOUR BADGE:

BE THE FIRST RAINBOW RANGER TO GET FROM ONE POINT TO ANOTHER POINT WITHOUT CHEATING.

BOMBASTIC BUGS
BADGE

HOW TO EARN YOUR BADGE:

FIND AND RECORD AT LEAST TEN TYPES OF BOMBASTIC BUG. BOMBASTIC BUGS ARE USUALLY POMPOUS IN ATTITUDE AND OFTEN CARRY A SMALL CANE.

FOOD THAT FARTS
BADGE

HOW TO EARN YOUR BADGE:

FIND FIVE EDIBLE SOURCES OF FOOD THAT FART. FARTS MUST BE LOUD AND SUSTAINED BUT NOT NECESSARILY SMELLY.

HOP UP THE MOUNTAIN
BADGE

HOW TO EARN YOUR BADGE:

MAKE YOUR WAY TO THE TOP OF THE HIGHEST MOUNTAIN BY HOPPING. ONLY ONE FOOT CAN TOUCH THE GROUND AT ALL TIMES.

CREATURES WITHOUT LEGS CAN USE ONE ARM. CREATURES WITH NO ARMS OR LEGS CAN USE THEIR HEAD.

FOOD FORAGING
BADGE

HOW TO EARN YOUR BADGE:

FIND ENOUGH EDIBLE SOURCES OF FOOD FROM YOUR NATURAL SURROUNDINGS TO SUSTAIN YOU FOR ONE WEEK.

BROKE A CURSE
BADGE

HOW TO EARN YOUR BADGE:

IF YOU HAPPEN TO BECOME CURSED . . . BREAK IT.

RAINBOW RANGER CAPTAIN
BADGE

HOW TO EARN YOUR BADGE:

AWARDED TO THE RAINBOW RANGER WHO EARNS THE MOST BADGES DURING THEIR CAMPING TRIP.

BUILD A SUMMER HOUSE FOR RICKY AND GRAHAM
BADGE

HOW TO EARN YOUR BADGE:

WORK AS A TEAM TO BUILD A SUMMERHOUSE BIG ENOUGH FOR TWO HANDSOME UNICORNS.

HOT TUB ENCOURAGED BUT NOT ESSENTIAL*

*GRAHAM SAYS IT IS ESSENTIAL.

FIND A LOST LEPRECHAUN *BADGE*

HOW TO EARN YOUR BADGE:

FIND A LOST LEPRECHAUN AND HELP HIM TO RETURN TO HIS BELOVED AND DANCE AROUND THE SUGARPLUM TREE ONCE AGAIN.

BE TINY AND BRAVE *BADGE*

HOW TO EARN YOUR BADGE:

WORK TOGETHER WITH FELLOW RANGERS TO SUCCESSFULLY SURVIVE CHALLENGING SITUATIONS SUCH AS RAIN, FLYING AND THE SEA ALL WHILE BEING THE SIZE OF A BUG.

SEA OF SPARKLES *BADGE*

HOW TO EARN YOUR BADGE:

EXPLORE AND ADAPT TO LIFE IN THE SEA OF SPARKLES.

SUPER DUPER TEAMWORK *BADGE*

HOW TO EARN YOUR BADGE:

AWARDED TO FOUR OF THE BRAVEST AND FRIENDLIEST CREATURES IN THE KINGDOM OF THE DARK AND THE LIGHT FOR WORKING TOGETHER AND NEVER GIVING UP HOPE.

THE RAINBOW RANGER PROMISE

IN THE BRIGHTEST DAY AND THE GLOOMIEST NIGHT,
WHETHER I'M A CREATURE OF DARK OR OF LIGHT.
I WILL BE PATIENT AND GRATEFUL AND KIND,
AND NEVER LEAVE A FELLOW RANGER BEHIND.
I'LL STRIVE TO KEEP LEARNING.
I'LL TREK AND EXPLORE,
AND PROMISE TO KEEP THE RAINBOW RANGER LAW.